CALAMITY FAIR

BOOKS BY WADE MILLER

Calamity Fair
Murder Charge
Shoot to Kill
Uneasy Street

CALAMITY FAIR

WADE MILLER

HarperPerennial
A Division of HarperCollins *Publishers*

This book was originally published in hardcover by Farrar, Straus & Cudahy in 1950. It is here reprinted by arrangement with Curtis Brown Ltd.

CALAMITY FAIR. Copyright © 1950 by Wade Miller. Copyright renewed © 1975 by Robert Wade and Enid A. Miller. All rights reserved. Printed in the United States of America. No part of this book may be used or reproduced in any manner whatsoever without written permission except in the case of brief quotations embodied in critical articles and reviews. For information address HarperCollins Publishers, Inc., 10 East 53rd Street, New York, NY 10022.

HarperCollins books may be purchased for educational, business, or sales promotional use. For information, please write: Special Markets Department, HarperCollins Publishers, Inc., 10 East 53rd Street, New York, NY 10022.

First HarperPerennial edition 1993.

Designed by George J. McKeon

Library of Congress Cataloging-in-Publication Data

Miller, Wade.
  Calamity fair/by Wade Miller.—1st HarperPerennial ed.
    p. cm.
  "Originally published in hardcover by Farrar, Straus & Cudahy in 1950."
  ISBN 0-06-097485-0 (paper)
  I. Title.
PS3563.I421475C34   1993
813'.54—dc20   92-53388

93 94 95 96 97 ❖/RRD 10 9 8 7 6 5 4 3 2 1

To Irene and Frank

CALAMITY FAIR

Chapter 1

SATURDAY, AUGUST 13, 6:00 P.M.

The tall man stopped running as soon as he had crossed the hot asphalt of Front Street, and skidded into the cool maw of the Greyhound Bus tunnel. With an effort, he forced his lean body to proceed at no more than a fast walk. Since no cry had been raised behind him, nobody paid him special attention. And, although his blue deep-set eyes darted from side to side, the rest of his gaunt hawk-nosed face remained set in impassive, almost bored, lines. He did not look like a fugitive.

The high concrete cave led through the city block behind the Pickwick Hotel. Passengers, porters, and drivers milled around the bus which would leave San Diego at six o'clock this afternoon but they each were intent on their own flustered affairs. They scarcely noticed the accused murderer who skirted that moment of their lives and kept going.

His name was Max Thursday. He rented an office—its glass door labeled Private Investigator—on the fourth floor of the Moulton Building, and a small duplex at the corner of Union and Ivy. He owned a car and a satisfactory bank account. But the maddening circumstances of this second Saturday in August had made it impossible for him to turn to any of these for rest or aid. He neither carried nor owned a gun.

Thursday hesitated as he reached the end of the Greyhound tunnel. The anger began to ebb from his mind, the fierce, blind temper that had led to his surprising assault on the law itself one minute before. He glanced both ways along First Avenue, trying to decide. He had constructed the trap for himself and he had escaped it momentarily. Foolishly or not, he was committed to a course of action all his own. What? Because any physical gesture was a balm, he fastened the button of his tweed coat, then unbuttoned it again, irresolute, wishing he could make himself think faster. Now that he was running away, he must run *to* somewhere.

He turned right simply because he noticed that Broadway—the honking neon-lit spine of San Diego—was filling with the beginnings of the Saturday evening trade. That struck a familiar note. The nebulous J. X. O'Connell had escaped earlier this week by vanishing into a throng on Broadway. He had escaped from Thursday who was now the pursued.

Two minutes gone. As he threaded among the slow-moving fun-seekers on the wide sidewalk, he became acutely conscious of passing time. He nearly could feel the watch spring expand and the minute hand advance over his left wrist. For the first time he noticed the innumerable clocks ticking away in the early-lighted store windows, and all their differing conceptions of time which was suddenly so important. He shook his head impatiently at the phobia and shoved ahead. Two minutes gone and it would take less than five minutes to get the man-wanted call on the police radio.

He longed to break into his sprint again. The absurd urge nagged Thursday, though he knew that no matter how fast he traveled he still was only wandering aimlessly.

Dodging around an arm-in-arm line of four marines, he teetered along the curb by the taxi stand at Second and Broadway. He hesitated again, then the readily opening door of the nearest car made him recall his instructions to Joaquin Vespasian the night before, ". . . wide the bus but no taxis. You won't be noticed on a bus and, besides, the bunch that's gunning for you owns a couple hack drivers."

For the next block, Thursday lengthened his stride. With no new implications, his own old advice seemed good enough to follow. Ahead, across Broadway, was the Plaza, the little green park that served as a terminal for the city bus system. He had at least decided on a method if not a destination.

As if that minor decision had freed his whole mind, he became aware of the passers-by. At first, he slowed his walk because he thought his fast pace was causing all the stranger faces with their eyes to turn toward him. Then he realized that he was becoming sensitive to the presence of others, as he had become conscious of his inexorable wrist watch. Behind him and to either side, he imagined the chatting, laughing voices called his name. Three minutes gone.

The Third Avenue traffic signal clanged and recolored, and he suddenly had to turn right again and cross Broadway instead. The sudden change nearly panicked him, the small matter of having to cross Broadway before crossing Third when he had expected otherwise. He felt exposed in the middle of the vast street with the cars halted, waiting for him alone to pass—it seemed—and the faces veiled behind windshields watching and commenting on his progress. He didn't dare hurry and he didn't dare not hurry.

He reached the curb finally, his clenched palms sweating, and prepared to wait for the signal to change again so he could get across Third to the Plaza. The corner was an arena, all eyes upon him. He had never fled from the law before. With nervous irritation, he glared around at the others trapped by the same red light and at the elderly newsboy who took it as an opportunity to proffer tomorrow morning's paper. Thursday muttered no, looked around again, and everybody's eyes slid away from his knowingly.

"Hi, Thursday!" The prowl car crawled across Broadway, losing speed just so one of the two uniformed men could yell at him. The policeman was Hoover, and Thursday had fresh memories of him from two encounters during this last unlucky week. But the prowl car wasn't going to stop, and Hoover merely grinned, so Thursday twisted his face into some sort of an expression in return. His name wasn't yet broadcast.

Thursday turned, with Hoover still looking at him, and sauntered into the drugstore. He hoped that would leave an impression that he wasn't vitally interested in the yellowish buses circulating around the Plaza like bees. By the magazine rack just inside the entrance, he spun and came out into the fading sunshine again and joined the pack that was walking into the green light.

He paused by the iron chain that fenced off the grassy park and couldn't locate a carrier that was going far enough to suit him. He wanted to go at least as far as one of the beaches or . . . Thursday began to run again—physically—toward the far end of the block. The sign on the bus idling there was the answer. It spelled out the one place remaining where he might be safe for a while.

But the bus doors were already closed and the driver shifted gears, ready to trundle off. Thursday yelled, "Hey!" and charged across Fourth Avenue against the light. The driver scowled but opened up and Thursday swung aboard. Four minutes gone.

Hat low over his coarse black hair, he slumped into a rear seat, anonymous. He caught his breath, and the engine vibrations, growling forward, made him feel temporarily free and better, as if in the little time he had left to him he might come up with something.

Since last Monday noon, two men had died by violence. He found it difficult to blame himself for that, no matter what the law said. But here he sat, hiding in awful aloneness, in flight from the law, and he knew he had himself chosen the tortuous route that led to this condition. Wearily, as he had before in the last six days, Thursday began to reconstruct. From the beginning. From last Monday noon when he had met Irene at the house in Loma Portal.

Chapter 2

MONDAY, AUGUST 8, 12:00 NOON

Max Thursday parked his Oldsmobile in front of the address on Azalea Drive, took the notebook from an inside pocket of his tweed coat and pretended to look up the number again, while he studied the house itself. He had a few minutes to spare before twelve noon. He had eaten an early Merchant's Monday Special in order to be in Loma Portal on the appointed hour.

He smiled, slightly but sincerely. The house pleased him; the neighborhood pleased him. In his profession, Thursday allowed himself the institutional ad in the telephone directory, and word of mouth was supposed to accomplish the rest. Words from mouths in this neighborhood would pay off. Loma Portal, its well-to-do residences rising suddenly on the rim of the mud flats northwest of San Diego, was the gateway to Point Loma and some still higher income brackets.

The house on Azalea Drive sat far back on a lawn between two rows of cypress. Its two-story, brown stucco front was bisected by a square tower in which the front door opened directly on the grass. Somehow, while Thursday was musing pleasurably, it had been opened without his seeing it at once, and a young woman stood there waiting.

He gave a quick nod and got out of his car, tucking the notebook away. Since the flagstones rambled, he cut straight across the lawn to her, his business smile in place. He didn't suppose she'd mind about the grass since it had evidently missed this week's mowing. Halfway to her, Thursday caught his toe in a small rectangular hole and stumbled. He silently thanked her for not laughing. She merely looked him over gravely.

In a clipped New England voice she stated a fact, "You're Mr. Thursday," and then added, "Come in, please do."

He took off his hat and said, "I generally manage a more impressive approach, Miss Whitney, but your gopher hole—" She was already across the tower foyer and one step down into the broad living room. He followed, trying to step on the scattered shag rugs rather than scratch her waxed floor. Two love seats confronted one another before the empty fireplace and she took the one which faced the bay-window view of the lawn. Thursday sat opposite her, looking as gentle and attentive as possible.

The woman was not as young as he had first thought, nearer his own age, thirty-five. She wore her slight air of arrogance like a perfume. She was poised and obviously well-bred, which pleased Thursday. She would have friends who might become worthwhile clients. Her small graceful body was dressed in a summerweight suit of powder-blue jersey and her dark blonde hair was drawn back tight to show off the lines of her face which was more patrician than pretty. Her one sign of any nervousness was the tensely drawn cords of her throat.

She said, in the clipped way he already liked, "As I told you, my name is Irene Whitney." Catching his glance at the indentation on her ring finger, she felt the need to explain something. "It's Miss Whitney now. I'm no longer married. I'm an interior decorator." She smiled just a little. "But neither of those points matter. I called you this morning because of— well, a gambling debt."

Thursday said, "In case you don't know, gambling debts aren't legally binding. If it's owed to you, I may be able to bluff the debtor into paying off. If it's owed by you, I can probably make sure you won't be bothered any more."

Irene Whitney shook her fine head impatiently. "No, I pay all my debts, Mr. Thursday. You see, I—" She took a deep breath for courage, her eyes, a paler blue than his own, still summing him up. He leaned back in the love seat so he wouldn't seem to hover over her personal secrets. He respected her for getting down to business this swiftly.

She said, without any coy pride in minor wickedness, "I've been doing some gambling over the past six months, mostly roulette. At first, I won a little but lately I've lost steadily. Quite a good deal. A thousand dollars. I gave him ten IOUs, a hundred dollars each. He—"

"Where'd you lose this money?"

"At a place called The Natchez. It's that place built out over the water at Mission Bay Park that looks like a showboat."

"I've been through it. Nightclub on the main deck. From there you take the elevator down for gambling or up for other accommodations. You went down."

Her pale-blue eyes glinted faint amusement. "I assure you I didn't know there was a choice until now."

"George Papago thinks he's quite a judge of character."

"Papago—he's the man who holds my IOUs." The cords of her throat tightened again. "Then you know him."

"Around and about. He wouldn't be such a bad guy if he could forget about angles. And he'd be better off." Thursday pulled a copy of the morning *Sentinel* from his coat pocket. He sprawled open the front page and ran his finger down through headlines. The finger passed across pictures of the Perry Showalter funeral and stopped on some black type farther down the page. Gambling "Ship" Operator Indicted By Grand Jury.

She barely glanced at it. "I knew The Natchez had been closed."

"Yes. It was closed when the state and our hard-working district attorney, Mr. Benedict, broke the syndicate. Papago thought he was smart enough to open it again. Now Mr. Benedict has broken him."

Irene Whitney eyed him oddly. Thursday smiled coldly, angry with himself. He realized some rancor had come into his voice when speaking of Benedict, and it wouldn't do to let this woman know he was on the wrong side of the district attorney.

He folded the paper noisily and said, "Well, I suppose the

point is that Papago holds your notes, and you want me to find him. He's out on bail. Have you tried his home? The paper gives his address as 709 Brighton Court, Mission Beach."

She shook her head again. "I haven't tried to find him. If it were that easy, I wouldn't have called you. You see, I'm being blackmailed."

"No, I hadn't seen that."

"Two days ago some woman telephoned me—it wasn't anyone I knew—and told me that I would have to pay for my IOUs. Of course I was willing to pay what I owed and I still am. But I can't afford to pay five thousand dollars to get my notes back. That's why I want your assistance."

"Go on."

She looked questioning.

"You've only told me half of it," Thursday said. "The woman must have said, 'or else.' She'd have to. Nobody would pay five thousand bucks to redeem a thousand-buck note unless there was a threat attached. What's the threat?"

She said blandly, "But I can't tell you that."

He shrugged. "That makes it a standoff. It's my job to respect your confidence and yours to supply it. Otherwise, I can't help you, Miss Whitney."

"Oh, come now." The arrogance peeped through her smiling disbelief. "There'll be a nice fee in it for you, Mr. Thursday."

He said abruptly, "Why did you call on me particularly?"

"Well—I've read about you in the papers—and—"

"Uh-huh. That was two years ago. Despite the exaggerations, I'm no stick-up man, and it seems to me that's what you're out to hire. I don't even own a gun, much less wear one. If you're interested in knowing, I work within the law and often with the law. The difference in my job is that I perform private services which the cops don't have the time or the right to perform. That's all a private detective amounts to, Miss Whitney."

She embarrassed him then by smiling at his speech. She said softly and knowingly, "I didn't intend to insult you, Mr. Thursday, and I don't ask you to act against whatever scruples you may have. But I would like you to see George Papago. I have reasons for not wanting to do it myself. Find out where my IOUs are and then redeem them for their full face value, no more. Is there anything dishonest in that?"

Thursday grinned. He liked her while he condemned his dangerous impulsiveness in liking her. But he did want her class of business. He said, "I'll see Papago this afternoon and find out just where your IOUs are. What's the number here—so I can call you about the money end?"

"I'll call you. Tomorrow sometime."

"Okay. My fee is twenty-five dollars per day plus unusual expenses, if they arise. The first day's fee is payable in advance."

"Oh, of course." She rose and went over to open the drawer of an escritoire. She returned, rummaging in her big purse for a wallet. Thursday saw the dark green of a checkbook.

"A check will do."

She pretended she didn't hear him. She held out two tens and a five and when he didn't take them immediately, she dropped them on the love seat beside him. Thursday ignored the money. He asked, "How are the Johnsons these days?"

She looked puzzled. He explained. "Your friends, the Johnsons. The people who let you use this house for our appointment. I checked Civic Center to see who owned this address. I also checked the registry of voters, the phone book, and the city directory. There's no Irene Whitney listed. I'm getting a strong hunch that isn't your name."

The woman let another five-dollar bill drip from her hand onto the love seat. She said, "Does it matter?"

Thursday picked up the thirty dollars. "Call my office in the morning. I'm there by nine." She snapped her purse shut, smiling confidently. He looked up at her. "You think you've got me tabbed, Miss Whitney. Don't forget I can drop anything I feel burning my hands. I have my own reasons for playing along."

"Fair enough." The cool assurance fled from her face as she stared past him, out the front window. Thursday twisted around. A portly, white-haired man had stopped part way up to the flagstones to the front door, his red face gazing benevolently around at the ragged lawn. Then he continued his advance on the house. "I didn't expect him," the woman whispered. "Put him off, please. Tell him I'm not here." She pushed gently at his shoulder.

Thursday shrugged and ambled to the door. When he opened it, the portly man frowned with surprise, then tugged down his vest and beamed rosily. "How do you do. I'm Bradstreet. How do you like it?"

"Fine." Thursday leaned across the doorway, indolently blocking it. "Can I do something for you?"

The other man blinked earnestly. Then his smile widened with tolerance. "I'm Bradstreet—Bradstreet Realtors. I guess this place sold itself to you. See you've taken the sign down." He gestured at the grass, toward the hole Thursday had stumbled over.

Slowly, Thursday eased out of the way. "Come in, I think there's some kind of mistake going on. You say nobody lives here?"

"Not since the Johnsons put it in our hands sixty days ago. What—"

"A Miss Whitney called me out here to make an estimate on a car. I haven't seen the car yet, but she's right inside. Or she was."

The two men circulated through the house. They found the sign behind the laundry tubs on the service porch, the sign that read For Lease Furnished—Call Bradstreet Realtors. Bradstreet carried it with him for the rest of the search. They wound up in the living room where he found the house key on the love seat by Thursday's hat. But the woman who claimed the name of Irene Whitney was gone.

"Nothing missing," Bradstreet said and wiped his face. "Don't get it. She looked reputable enough. I let her have the key about ten this morning so she could brood around the place, get the feel of it, make up her mind. You know women. Then, when I saw you I assumed I'd misheard her give her name. Thought she had a husband and you were it."

"Might have been some confidence setup or maybe she was just playing rich," Thursday said affably. "Did you see this car I was supposed to look at?"

"Didn't notice." Bradstreet led the way out the front door, locked it and rattled it viciously. "Fine place but we're asking six prices for it. And just when I thought I had a sucker to unload it on . . ." He stabbed his sign into its hole and used his weight to force it deeper. "One thing I should've learned by now. Never trust a blonde, age and respectability notwithstanding. They'll lie to you every time."

"Keeps a man on his toes," Thursday said and walked out to his car. He felt sure she hadn't been lying completely. Besides, he argued himself down, I owe her something for her money.

Chapter 3

MONDAY, AUGUST 8, 2:00 P.M.

Mission Beach was the flat spit of land which divided the sparkling ocean surf from the placid bay. On both sides of the amusement park, the sandy lots were dotted with beach homes of white stucco and red tile roofs; 709 Brighton Court was one of these at the south end.

The front door was open and through the screen Thursday could see the empty living room as he punched the bell. Some child's toys lay around the carpet and three punctured beer cans sat on the coffee table.

Out of sight he could hear George Papago and a woman quarreling at the top of their lungs, but he couldn't distinguish words. At his hip a thin voice said, "You know where you can go."

Thursday looked down. A soiled, homely boy of about five had crept around the corner of the house and up onto the concrete stoop. He was skinny, big-eyed, and sallow despite the blazing sun. "Hi," Thursday said. "I'm looking for Mr. Papago. Does he live here?"

The boy brushed by into the house and let the screen slam between them. He stood inside, his mouth hanging open, staring at the tall man. When Thursday punched the bell again, he piped helpfully, "It don't work."

Papago yelled from somewhere in the rear, "Georgie! Who you talking to?"

The boy flinched. "Just a man, Daddy! He looks like a cop!"

"Huh?" Papago padded into the living room, the olive skin of his face and neck flushed with irritation. He was a slick young Greek with clever eyes and a black line of mustache. He wore green slacks, open-toed sandals, and a blue sport shirt buttoned at the throat in spite of the heat. He calmed down a little when he saw his visitor, asked him in and offered him a beer.

Thursday said no, thanks. Papago got one for himself in the kitchen, chased the gaping Georgie out of the living room and sank moodily onto the davenport. "What you doing these days, Thursday?"

"This and that. Reading about you in the paper mostly."

"You wouldn't be working for the D.A. now, would you?" When Thursday laughed, Papago said, "Glad to see somebody who isn't. All I meet any more are Benedict's boys, trying to sew me up tight."

"How bad have they got you, George?"

"Could be worse. I'll get off with a fine, says my lawyer." He gulped off most of the beer. "That cold fish Benedict acts like I slew the mayor or some such stunt. What did I do so wrong? Sure, my setup was against the law, but what isn't these days? People got to do something, entertain themselves somehow, don't they?"

"Sure." Thursday listened for the woman he knew was in the house but he couldn't hear her.

Papago snarled on about his troubles. "That's what's losing my mind for me! Waiting for the trial to get over, so I'll be free to open up in some other line. You might know how a thing like this louses up your credit."

In the distance, an ice-cream wagon tinkled. Immediately, Georgie scampered in from the bedroom, shouting, "Give me a nickel! Give me a nickel!"

"Shut up!" Papago yelled. "Can't you see I'm talking?"

The boy said stubbornly, "Mommy said for you to give me a nickel."

Papago swore and finally dug out some coins and gave one to Georgie who banged out through the front screen. "That kid can hear the Good Humor wagon a mile off. He can't hear me across the room." He dropped the loose change back in his pocket and fiddled with a torn pamphlet that he had pulled out with the money.

Thursday figured it was a horoscope from the zodiacal symbols he could see on the cover. "You looking for lucky days?"

"Me?" Papago scornfully tossed the pamphlet on the coffee table in front of him. "What's the scoop on you, Thursday? You didn't stock up on crying towels just because the D.A. has me across the barrel."

"Always glad to see Benedict pick on somebody else for a change." Thursday grinned. "But you're right, George. I got business."

"Righto. Name it."

"I have a client, a Miss Irene Whitney. She's an interior decorator, just gotten a big commission back in New York. Happened all of a sudden when—but that doesn't matter to you. The point is that she's had to leave town in a hurry and she hired me to wind up her affairs."

Papago was intent with curiosity. "I don't get it."

"Well, the list of business she gave me had your name on it. She owes you some notes on dough she dropped at The Natchez. Five hundred bucks."

"You got that wrong. It was a thousand. A hundred ten times."

"You're probably right. I have it written down somewhere. Anyway, she wants me to pay up for her."

"You still got your wires crossed, Thursday," said Papago. "Those IOUs were picked up last week by her lawyer. Course, I don't mind getting paid twice if she don't mind." He laughed until he noticed Thursday's probing eyes. "What's the matter? If anybody's thrown you a curve, it wasn't me."

Thursday grimaced. "Wasted my time coming out here, that's all. The Whitney woman must have forgotten about it in the rush. Her lawyer, huh? You mean Fisher—young fellow, dark hair."

Papago laughed at him again. "You even got the wrong lawyer. This was a tall character—like you—by name of J. X. O'Connell. Know him? Gray hair and cookie duster. The Harris-tweeds and walking-stick type."

"Oh, O'Connell, sure. George, do you happen to have his address handy?"

Papago said, "Wouldn't be surprised," then his eyes narrowed calculatingly. "Don't you have it?"

"Back at the office someplace. I figured you could save me a trip back downtown."

"Righto," said the gambler thoughtfully. "I get it."

A long-legged, husky woman strode in from the bedroom, smiling self-consciously. Her brown eyes were set wide apart, like an animal's, in a heavy-boned face. For all her large scale, she was sensually handsome. The brown hair that hung down the back of her gold blouse had just been carefully brushed, and Thursday realized why she hadn't shown up before. She had been dressing up for company in black hostess pajamas and gold sandals. He rose politely.

Papago stayed where he was and said indifferently, "Nell. Max Thursday."

She shook Thursday's hand and asked how he'd been in a healthy voice. Then she looked at Papago finishing his beer. "Say, why can't all of us have a beer together?"

Papago set the empty can down with a crash. "What do you think, I got no manners? He don't want a beer!"

"How was I to know, tell me that!"

"If somebody don't want something, I don't force it or me down their throat. Like some people I could name."

"What do you want me to do all my life—stay in the bedroom?" Nell snapped and the glow in her dull eyes dared him to answer. She wheeled on Thursday, winningly. "Wouldn't you really like a beer, Mr. Thursday?"

Thursday smiled and said, "I don't want to start a war. Or let you drink alone, either. You decide."

Nell was loftily triumphant as she returned from the kitchen to distribute three foaming cans of beer. Then she spotted the horoscope pamphlet Papago was toying with again.

"Hey!" she cried, "so that's where it was! You've gone and torn it!"

Papago pulled the horoscope out of her reach and tore it again, deliberately. "And that's what'll happen to any more I find around here, too."

Nell's stormy reply was lost in the slam of the screen door as Georgie trotted back into the house, his tongue working over a chocolate ice-cream cone. Papago growled, "And don't drip that thing on the rug."

"Come here, honey." Nell soothed the youngster against her leg and petted his hair.

Thursday tossed off the rest of his beer. "About that O'Connell's address, George," he prompted.

"Righto," said the Greek. His eyes rested thoughtfully on Georgie's ice-cream cone. He laid the ripped horoscope in front of him on the coffee table. Then he got out his wallet and extracted a business card from it. He put the card down by the horoscope, glanced up to see if Thursday was ready and read off the address—"3319 30th Street."

"I thought it was some building downtown."

Nell started to speak and then changed her mind. Thinking clumsily, she watched Papago, and Thursday watched them both. The gambler replaced the card in his wallet. Then he balled the horoscope and flung it into a corner.

Nell didn't explode as Thursday expected. She remained contemplative. Thursday got up and added his empty to those on the coffee table. "Thanks a million, George. Good luck with the D.A."

"Righto," Papago said absently, not rising. "See you around."

Nell followed him to the door, Georgie clinging to a fold of pajama leg. "So glad to make your acquaintance. Drop around any time, now you know the way."

Thursday thanked her, bid the chocolate-mouthed youngster goodbye and went out to his car. At the next intersection of the main thoroughfare, Mission Boulevard, he pulled off the road and parked behind a garage.

He didn't have to wait long. Within five minutes a Chrysler Town and Country convertible coupe shot by him, headed south toward downtown. George Papago's scheming face was behind the wheel. He had added a sport coat to his ensemble and a green panama hat with a wide flowered band. The flashy Chrysler was out of sight around the corner of the garage before Thursday could get the license number.

Thinking over the thousand-and-one stunts which Papago might be up to, Thursday drove back to San Diego and stopped at an Owl drugstore. Again, he checked through the phone book and the city directory.

There was no such person as J. X. O'Connell. He was the second nonexistent person who had turned up today.

Chapter 4

MONDAY, AUGUST 8, 3:30 P.M.

Thursday checked the 30th Street address as a matter of routine. This fringe of the North Park suburb was loosely a business district: homes elbowed other homes which had been converted into shoe-repair shops and dressmaking establishments.

Number 3319 existed. It was an ice-cream cone, upside down.

The stucco cone, three stories high, was one of those depression-built refreshment stands which housed one enterprise after another, down through the years. Apparently, coats of whitewash kept the flimsy, pointed structure from falling apart. High on its tip, another ice-cream cone, this of fraying plaster and right-side up and a mere yard long, still balanced like a dancer.

Thursday chuckled as, parked by the curb, he traced the workings of Papago's mind. He read the metal sign swinging over the shabby lawn. JOAQUIN VESPASIAN, Personal Relations Counsellor. In smaller letters this was explained: Phrenologist, Spiritual Consultant, Your Personality As Revealed By Your Palm, Helpful Secrets Of The Egyptians, Handwriting Analyzed. Then, challengingly: Why Not Meet The Real You?

"Tightrope walker," Thursday murmured. A history of local legislation was layered in the sign. The Future Foretold had been painted over long ago when the city banned fortune-telling. More recently, Psychologist had been obliterated when requirements were tightened.

Inside the cone somebody shrieked.

Thursday shut off his engine and sprinted up to the door in the circular base of the building. He stopped outside the wedged-open door and stayed there, since the fight going on inside was none of his business.

The two big men in dungarees were of Italian or Portuguese descent. Even knotted in anger, their swarthy faces looked like the same family. One was older and slower than the other.

They swore in growls as they knocked a little plaid-suited man around the dinky room. The little man whimpered and didn't do much fighting. He kept his face covered and tried to run away but the other two always caught him, knocking him against the wall with roundhouse swings. The victim wasn't being hurt so badly, that Thursday could see, despite his noises. Thursday went back out to his car to lean against it and light a cigarette.

A few more crashing sounds and the two swarthy men stomped out, glowered at Thursday as they passed and drove away in a battered pickup truck. Thursday went into the ice-cream cone and looked around.

The front half of the building was a cheaply furnished consultation room with a large round table, some chairs which Thursday set up again, cupboards, and two display cases. One case featured magic tricks—"Fool Your Friends"; the other glass box showed off twisted roots and various statuettes, charms which "The Ancients Superstitiously Believed Would Bring Luck—Are You Lucky Enough?" Some dingy prayer rugs were kicked around on the floor, and the walls were hung occasionally with imitation-silk shawls of Chinese design.

The rear half of the building seemed to be divided into two smaller rooms, a bedroom and a hotplate kitchen. The little man came out of the bedroom nervously, brushing off his plaid trousers. He had put a salve on one side of the low forehead where the swelling had started.

To Thursday's grin, he responded sullenly with, "Two of them, you notice. One of them couldn't have done it." Then he opened a cupboard, said, "Well, a little of the old tonic," and upended a bottle briefly. He didn't offer Thursday a drink.

Joaquin Vespasian was small, five-six, but proportionate.

Only his shifty eyes were full-size, which gave him a wise smirking look. With his round face and plastered-down hair nearly the same shade of tan, he reminded Thursday of the bronze owl trademarks in the drugstore he had just left. He represented a cheaper, gaudier edition of the George Papago class. Too many rings glittered on his stubby grasping hands.

"Since you're looking so curious," said Vespasian, "that last performance was put on by the Lalli family. Rosa comes here for personality adjustments and invaluable self-knowledge. Her father and brother have got dirty suspicious minds. Now what can I do for you?"

"About that self-knowledge." Thursday tried a shot in the dark. "You're getting into deep trouble."

"Not me." Vespasian folded a stick of gum, fit it into his mouth and chewed knowingly. "They didn't find Rosa here, did they?" He winked and jerked a thumb toward his back door. "Bus line just one-half block away."

"I don't care about your girl troubles. How about this other? Who's this J. X. O'Connell going around buying up other people's gambling debts?"

"Brother, you're shaking the wrong tree."

Thursday had figured he was, but he remained lounging solemnly against the edge of the round table while Vespasian swaggered around the office, straightening it up some. Thursday watched him chew his gum and turn over ways to make a fast buck out of this.

"On the other hand, maybe you got something," Vespasian said suddenly, and Thursday nearly laughed. "First, I'd have to know your angle."

Thursday held out one of his cards for the little man to read.

"Glad to meet you, Maxie. Who's your principal?"

"I'm my principal. Don't keep the card."

"Why not? You want to find a guy. I might call you with something."

"You won't call me with anything. And I don't want my card found on your body."

Vespasian said suspiciously, "What kind of a threat is that?"

"Not any kind. Put me down as quaint. I try not to leave my cards with finaglers because they come to such bad ends."

"Now, let's not be hasty. Who's your client?"

"Let's not be funny."

"Look, Maxie"—Vespasian put a confidential hand on Thursday's elbow—"we're both smart enough to know the private cop business is based on contact work. Now this setup I got might not look like much to a big fellow like you but things drift through here, little things you might use." When he got to selling, Vespasian talked in a breathless, yapping voice like a terrier. "Of course, I don't pretend that this crystal-ball pitch is anything but the old fakeroo."

"No kidding?"

"Sure thing. Lay a soothing hand on the worried lady's forehead and she's sold—for money. I get along. You know that, your racket's pretty much the same, isn't it? Now, I'm one of the finest little contacts you could make, Maxie. You can ask them down at the police department, go ahead. They'll tell you I'm inside and often. How about it?"

"How about what?"

"A small down payment makes a working agreement between us."

Thursday pulled out his wallet and glanced into it casually. Vespasian chewed his gum faster. Thursday said, "I may have an angle myself."

"What's that?"

"That you stand a better chance of running across J. X. O'Connell if I tip you afterwards." He put his wallet away and buttoned his hip pocket.

"You know it, Maxie. I see we think the same way. J. X. O'Connell? He's your boy."

Thursday was obliged to shake his damp little hand.

"By the by," Vespasian asked as if it had barely occurred to him, "what brought you around to me?"

"A good friend of yours. George Papago."

Vespasian screwed up his face, confused.

Thursday said, "Our mutual friend George wanted to hand me a phony address for one reason or another. Right at that time he was playing with one of your horoscopes. When his kid walked in licking an ice-cream cone, this place came to mind. So he read me your address off the horoscope instead of the one I wanted."

"Well, well. You're quite an operator yourself, Maxie."

"Thanks. The joker is that the address George held back is also a phony."

Vespasian smiled innocently. "Just who's this George? I don't believe I know him."

"That's kind of weird. You're selling your goods to his girl friend Nell. I think George is another one with a dirty suspicious mind."

"Oh, Nell Kopke! And George Papago. I didn't get his name the first time."

"Sure not. Where's your phone?" Vespasian showed him into the rumpled bedroom. Thursday looked up the Papago number and rang the house in Mission Beach. Nell answered with an angry hello.

Thursday said gruffly, "This is Charley. George around?" Somewhere around town, Papago would know a Charley.

Nell said, "No, he's not here, Charley. The slob took off an hour ago to get drunk. I don't know when he'll be back. And I don't much care."

"Okay, thanks." Thursday hung up and frowned at the pinup calendar over the bed. Papago hadn't returned yet. He might have stayed out to look for J. X. O'Connell. Obviously, he had sensed something profitable in Irene Whitney's IOUs.

By Thursday's elbow, Vespasian wasn't missing a thing. "Maxie, you're baffled. I think I got the answer. You—"

"I'm often baffled." Thursday said. "It comes of being born under a question mark."

Chapter 5

MONDAY, AUGUST 8, 7:00 P.M.

He thought it over a long time, stirring a cup of coffee in a drive-in, wondering whether the case was worth pushing. The presence of two nonexistent persons in it both intrigued Thursday and cautioned him. He called Papago's house again—as Charley—and Nell Kopke said that George hadn't returned. That was at five o'clock and made it even more probable that Papago was still looking for J. X. O'Connell or had found him.

Still telling himself he wasn't certain he wanted to mix in this, Thursday called the city's two leading job printing plants where he had contacts. No one answering Papago's description had tried to run down O'Connell through his faked business card. That was the logical, foot-aching method, the sort of method which wouldn't appeal to George Papago.

The Bureau of Motor Vehicles was closed by now and there was no exact way to procure the license number of Papago's Chrysler. However, he could still keep an eye out for a flashy convertible. When that thought came to Thursday, he knew his curiosity was replacing his better sense—as it had with Irene Whitney. He gave in. He would wander around town, hoping to cross the gambler's trail. Papago was the nearest link to his fictitious client's fictitious attorney.

Thursday caught a quick sandwich for dinner and drove

downtown. A navy port, a tourist resort—San Diego had more than its share of bars. It was now seven o'clock and it was in the bars that Papago's circle of acquaintances would be appearing from nowhere and preparing to operate. But where to start?

Arbitrarily, he began looking along Market Street in the neighborhood of the Bridgway Hotel, the shady flophouse where he had undergone the rocky days after the war. He drifted from bar to bar, not drinking, only ordering a cheap beer when the bartender appeared unco-operative. Occasionally he greeted customers or waiters whom he knew and who served as tipsters for his agency. He learned nothing. After an hour he swung north to F Street where swarms of white-capped sailors crowded Patrick's and the Rainbow Gardens and lined up before the burlesque theater.

At the Camelot, he picked up the first trace of the gambler.

"George?" said the barhop, sorting her change. "Yeah, he was in a while back, looking for somebody. Guess it must have been you, huh, bud?"

The trail got warm through three successive F Street places. But the answers were the same in all of them: "Sure, he was here, had a shot and shoved off." Except that he had predicted Papago's methods exactly, Thursday's hunt was failing. He was running a full hour behind the gambler.

At ten o'clock he stooped out of the phone booth of the Aces Up and sauntered through the jukebox din back to his untasted beer. He had just called the Papago house again. No answer; now Nell was out also. With the Aces Up, Thursday had canvassed all of the bars south of Broadway. Which direction had the gambler taken? Uptown, the waterfront, or toward the suburbs?

The bartender waddled down to Thursday's corner of the bar. He filled a tray with sparkling needles of shattered ice and picked up their previous fruitless conversation, taking a new tack. "You say you're a friend of Papago's?"

"Same sorority."

The bartender looked him over. "Well, you might do him a favor if you felt like it." Thursday raised his eyebrows. The bartender laid a gold cigarette lighter on the hardwood. "That's the Greek's. He left it here when he was in. George was pretty well flying tonight."

Thursday smiled ruefully. He could believe that. He felt bloated himself just from sitting over beers. If Papago had downed a drink in each bar . . . "You'll probably see him before I will," he said. "I been hoping I'd catch up with him, but—" He shrugged.

The bartender tossed the lighter on a lower shelf. "Well, I tried. I ran after him but he'd already gunned out in that fancy bus of his and he didn't hear me yell, I guess. I hate to get stuck with customers' jewelry."

"George is a hard man to make listen," Thursday said. Then, "Which way'd he go—or did you notice?"

"Up Third. The Pickwick, the Frémont, that neck of the woods. Hey, anything wrong with the beer?"

Thursday strode directly to his parked sedan, beginning to enjoy the warm night air. He laughed at his own rationalization. When luck was good, he called it brains; when it went against him, it was nothing but bad luck. He drove up Third Avenue to Broadway and the cluster of big downtown hotels: San Diego, Pickwick, John C. Frémont, and U. S. Grant. As he circled their blocks, he scanned the lines of parked cars on both sides of the street.

In less than five minutes of searching, he located a Chrysler Town and Country convertible that looked like the gambler's. It was parked as if for display under a street light at the corner of Third and B. Thursday pulled into the loading zone directly behind it and got out. He kicked himself mentally for not thinking of getting the license number early enough.

A glance around and he sauntered up to the empty convertible and tried the door. It was locked. The registration slip was buckled around the steering post but it was in shadow.

Thursday flattened his face against the glass to peer at it.

A heavy voice behind him said, "What's the trouble here, fellow?"

Thursday straightened and smiled at the young patrolman who had come around the corner. "Evening, officer. I was just trying to satisfy my curiosity."

"Your car or not?"

"No." Thursday sighed. "Wish it were. You see, I've been thinking of buying a new one and these Chryslers kind of interest me. I was sneaking a look at the inside."

The big young policeman, looking uncomfortable in his new uniform, studied Thursday. Finally, "Okay. You've had your look."

"Take it easy," Thursday said amiably and walked on. He wanted to stay near Papago's car and wait for the gambler to return. But not with the suspicious rookie in the neighborhood.

Instead, he returned to touring the bars. The Jade, Club Royal, Cuckoo Club, Stork Club, Gold Rail . . . Papago's tipsy condition had left a plain trail down Third Avenue. These were glossier places than the ones earlier, more officers and petty officers, more neckties. The time gap had been cut down to a half hour.

Thursday sped up his search. He sensed that he was closing in and he stepped in and out of nightclubs, asking brief questions but mainly looking for the Greek's face. He had nearly completed the circuit of drinking spots within walking distance of the Chrysler when the chase ended—but without George Papago. At a quiet, knotty-pine bar, McCloskey's Shining Hour, the sallow bartender remembered him clearly.

"That's the lad, all right," he told Thursday. "I thought I recognized him from the papers or somewhere. He pulls up a stool alongside a tall gentleman with gray hair who had a scotch-and here at the bar. They had a talk."

"This gentleman a good dresser?" Thursday asked. Inside,

he was feeling hollow. He had lost his evening-long race with Papago. Once the gambler and O'Connell got their heads together, the picture was bound to get complicated. "Mustache—walking stick—that sort of thing?"

"That's it. It was the walking stick that made me notice him—like some character out of the *Esquire* ads. You know."

"Happen to hear what they were talking about?"

"Not me, mister," the bartender said stiffly. "I make it a rule not to butt in unless I'm asked to butt in." He got friendly again. "Anyway, they didn't stay long enough. Your lad with the load—what'd you say the slick one's name was?—he wanted to shove off somewhere, I think."

Thursday blew out his breath, telling himself it didn't matter as much as he was making out. But it was irritating to lose a race. His disappointment must have showed through because the bartender said solicitously, "Wanted to see them tonight, eh?"

"About a job," Thursday agreed absently.

"Well, you might get it if you hurried. They went out, oh, at least twenty minutes ago. Then the old guy came back in and made a phone call from that booth. If they're walking they can't have gotten far." The bartender shook his head. "And the lad certainly wasn't in any shape for driving."

Thursday planted a dollar on the bar and plunged out under the street lights again. He ran down the sidewalk, heading for Papago's car. He rounded the corner and stopped.

The convertible was gone. For a moment, he relieved his feelings by swearing viciously. Then he laughed softly at himself. He had used up all the luck he deserved by tracking the gambler as far as he had. Tomorrow he could start dealing with Papago on a new basis.

He had left his own car unlocked. He walked around in the street and got into the driver's seat. His hand reached the key halfway to the ignition when he saw what lay beside him. The light from the street lamp flung a glowing, oblong pattern across the front seat. And framed in the light was a green panama hat with a wide flowered band.

The crown had been crushed. Gingerly, Thursday lifted it, keeping his fingers away from the dark wet stains. He made sure none of the blood had come off on the upholstery. Stamped into the sweatband were the initials he expected: G.P.

He laid the hat down again, carefully. He meditated, staring out through the windshield at the intersection and the neon signs that still offered entertainment down the avenue. For some reason, George Papago had been put out of the picture. Thursday shook his head; he had expected complications from the gambler but not this one. Papago had drunk too much, he had driven too sharp a bargain with . . . well, presumably the shadowy J. X. O'Connell.

But why had the hat been left in Thursday's car? A warning? Or a trap?

Either way, it angered him. Either way, it added up to a challenge. Somebody—O'Connell, whatever his name was—was getting clever with him. Thursday scowled and skinned his lips back over his teeth.

The proper place for the crushed hat right now was the police department. He could turn it in and start unwinding his explanations about his client with the phony name and about his unsuccessful chase through most of the bars. He would have to explain several times, finally to the district attorney himself. After that, at the luckiest, he would get lectured and blocked out of the Whitney-Papago-O'Connell case for good.

His smile was grim as he kicked the engine to life and pulled away from the curb. There were three persons who, on the surface, knew of his connection with this case. Nell, Papago's mistress—his common-law widow now, most likely. The so-called Irene Whitney—whereabouts unknown. And

Joaquin Vespasian, the annoying little sharper who had been dragged across the path as a red herring by Papago.

"Well, you never know," Thursday mused.

It was considerably out of his way going home, but he drove out to 30th Street where the whitewashed ice-cream cone loomed ghostly against the night sky. Meticulously and silently, Thursday hung Papago's smashed panama on the front doorknob. Then he went home to wait for the next move.

CHAPTER 6

TUESDAY, AUGUST 9, 9:00 A.M.

He could find nothing in the morning papers, *Union* or *Sentinel*, relating to George Papago. He ate breakfast in the waffle shop near the Moulton Building and rode up to his fourth-floor office shortly after nine o'clock.

"Hey! Maxie!" Joaquin Vespasian hovered and fidgeted outside his office door. His fingertips looked damp, as if he had been biting his nails. But he mustered a sickly, smart-aleck grin for Thursday. "Didn't I tell you to leave it to me? Brother, I got something!"

Thursday nodded gravely, spun his keys around his finger and didn't unlock the door. "What besides the jitters?"

"Inside," Vespasian advised and winked. Under one arm, rumpling his cheap pin-stripe suit, he lugged a cardboard hatbox.

Thursday opened for business. He took his time adjusting the venetian blinds, and the little man shifted his feet impatiently.

Thursday asked, "Okay, what?"

Vespasian set the hatbox on the desk importantly but kept a hand on the lid. "What's it worth?"

"I got a hat. Not interested."

"Don't joke, Max. This is big. I want a cut."

"I'd have to see it."

Vespasian swept the lid off the box with a flourish. Thursday lifted out the green panama between thumb and forefinger. The bloodstains had dried darkly, patterning the battered rear of the hat. Papago had been snapped from behind.

Thursday sank into his swivel chair and stared calmly across the desk at Vespasian. But he had begun to seethe inside. He had never liked George Papago or his kind. But, even with the gambler drunk, the murderer hadn't had guts enough to risk a frontal attack. And now Vespasian had come to sell the dead man's hat. Thursday stared at him, feeling unclean himself, remembering last night how clever he had considered Max Thursday who made chess moves with the victim's clothes.

Vespasian sidled into the client chair and said nervously, "Well?"

Thursday snapped, "Where'd this come from?"

"Surely you recognize it?"

"Nothing sure about it. I saw one like it yesterday and that's all."

"But the initials—G.P.—here on the band?" Vespasian's stubby forefinger shook as he pointed. "George Papago. What do you say to that?"

"What do you say? That you killed him?"

"No, no! Look." Vespasian jumped out of the chair and leaned across the desk. "I'm doing you the favor, Max. You know my business setup; I live there, too. When I got up this morning and opened the front door, I found this hat lying just outside. The color—and then the initials—it's pretty distinctive. It couldn't belong to anyone else but Papago."

Thursday dug a battered pack of Raleighs out of a drawer and lit up. "Get to the point. Get to me."

"You? Why, Papago played a dirty trick of some sort on you yesterday afternoon. Now something's happened to him. As a friend, I risked my tail bringing that thing up here to you. I want to get together. What's it worth?"

"Thanks, friend," Thursday murmured. For a moment, he watched the cigarette smoke coil up. Then he said, "Let's play that back again. Vespasian, in your business you would have an afternoon and evening trade—not a morning trade. Another fact: cheap operators like you always sleep in the mornings. I never saw a sharp boy yet that didn't have a sense of luxury. So—what were you doing up early enough to find that hat before the paper boy or the milkman? What are you doing up this early right now?"

Vespasian's round tan face paled a little but he managed to smirk. He sat down again, watchfully. "Okay. I missed that point, didn't I? Here's the way it really was. I didn't spend most of the night in *my* bed. When I got home—it was about three—I found that thing hanging on my front doorknob. Except for that, the rest of it's true, believe me."

"I'm not going to," Thursday said flatly. "You didn't dash up to see me because I might be in trouble. You thought you might be in trouble."

"Okay, have it your way." Vespasian chewed his lip sullenly. "We'll forget the money angle this time. The hat makes it look like Brother Papago came to a pretty rough end. Well, Papago dropped around to my place a couple days back and told me off. He didn't like me—ah—handling his Nell's business."

"What's one more jealous husband on your long list?"

"Listen, when a character gives my address to promote some deal and that same night his bloody hat is hung on my door, why, even I get a little jumpy. And I been around, Maxie." His own eyes half-closed wisely. "I thought you'd want in on the free-for-all."

"So your story is that you're being framed."

"Got a better one? Otherwise..."

"No alibi for last night."

Vespasian winked. "She'd never admit it."

"Put me down for a copy of your memoirs when you find time to write them. Those I want to read."

"I keep busy," Vespasian said comfortably.

"Busy lying. An honest man would have taken that hat straight to the cops."

"Frankly, Maxie, I wouldn't know."

Despite himself, Thursday laughed. Then he stood up. "Grab your hat," he said, "and let's go."

"I take it you're representing me. About the finances—"

"Nope. All I'll do is chaperone you down to police headquarters."

Vespasian blinked. "Wait—a—minute!"

"Where'd you park your car?"

"Now, wait a minute. What you pulling? I gave you that dope in confidence. You can't run me in after—"

"Relax. I'm returning your favor, Vespasian. If you're telling the truth, you're in the clear. If you're not, I can't pull you out anyway. You tell your story to Lieutenant Clapp. That way, you'll be covered if anything does pop on the Papago business."

"Oh." Vespasian caught on. "Connections?"

Thursday nodded and herded the little man ahead of him. They drove to the foot of Market Street in Vespasian's faded Ford sedan, left it in the police parking lot and tramped into the restful corridors of the headquarters, a low, tile-roofed Spanish building that enclosed a flowered patio. Clapp was out and they sat on a hard antiqued bench outside his office, waiting. Thursday smoked in thoughtful silence but Vespasian drummed his fingers on the hatbox and tried to make conversation.

A half hour droned by before the homicide chief's big body blocked the sunny entrance. He was tired and rumpled but plainly pleased with the world as he strode down the hall. "Up since three on a murder," he told Thursday as they all settled around his tiny office. Austin Clapp had a heavy face, tanned and shrewd, beneath a dappled crop of gray-and-brown hair. He kept scratching his unshaven jaw, and his eyes, blood-shot this morning, idly dissected Vespasian.

"Anyone we know?" Thursday asked casually. Vespasian's fingers beat a quicker tattoo on the hatbox.

"I doubt it. A carhop out at one of the El Cajon drive-ins. Knifed her and dumped her down a canyon. A male hair on her shoulder where some guy had laid his head. Spectrum showed lead filings on the hair. So when we hauled in her boy friends we landed a steamfitter. He still had the jack-knife on him." Clapp loaded the pipe Thursday had given him last Christmas and sighed happily through the smoke cloud. "I wish they all got over in seven hours. Well, what trouble you in now, Max?"

"Haven't classified it yet." Thursday took the hatbox from Vespasian. "Mr. Vespasian here wishes to bring forth some evidence in what he believes may be a homicide case. In exchange, of course, he's looking for evidentiary immunity, which I told him you could fix."

"Um," grunted Clapp and his steel-gray eyes drilled through Vespasian. "Let's have it."

Vespasian glanced at Thursday, who nodded. Vespasian began talking rapidly, occasionally stammering. He repeated the story he had told Thursday, the final version.

After Clapp had looked over the bloodstained panama, he asked gently, "And why did you go to Thursday with this instead of to us?"

"Just a mistake. I got confused and didn't use the old head," Vespasian said. "Maxie and I being old friends back in Denver and him being a—"

"That's right, Clapp," Thursday cut in smoothly. "Vespasian did a foolish thing, he realizes that, but most people do when something like this comes up. I steered him right down here."

Clapp grunted again and ran his tongue across his teeth. "Well, let's have your full name, address, and phone," he ordered Vespasian and wrote them down. "That's fine and dandy, Mr. Vespasian. We appreciate your coming down here."

Vespasian popped out of his chair, wiping his hands on his flashy suit. "I guess I'm free to go?"

"As a bird. We'll want you handy if anything does come of this matter, so stick around town." Clapp smiled his friendly smile. "Otherwise, don't worry."

Vespasian grinned and nodded, winked at Thursday and slid out of the office like a minnow. There was a silence after the door drifted shut. Then Clapp said softly, "Now just what the heck was that pig Latin about evidentiary immunity—Maxie?"

Thursday laughed. "How would he know you're an honest man? I had to spin something to get him down here. Otherwise, he might have just burned up the hat and you'd never have seen it."

"Why didn't he anyway? He's the type."

"Beats me. He came sucking around me with that leaky story. I though the smart thing would be to set it up so he could still run around. That's your own method, as I remember. The pass-out-rope method."

"Your compliments always mean an angle. What's this one?"

Thursday met his eyes easily. "No angle. Just a favor for a buddy."

"Uh-huh." Clapp scratched his beard and grinned. "George Papago was a boy for angles, too." He grinned broader at another thought. "And if Papago has gone under, I'd like to see Benedict's face. He was going to make quite a lesson out of that gambling trial."

Thursday yawned openly.

Clapp murmured, "Just *you* stay clear of Benedict, son."

"Sure, Clapp. When does he start leaving me alone?"

"Remember he's as honest as you or me. You two are just different types that ought to avoid each other. He's the type that's so honest he's almost vindictive. And you *do* have four killings to your credit. All legal, of course, but . . . "

Thursday gazed out at the sun-wilted flowers in the patio. After a moment, he shrugged and smiled wryly. "Well, I've lived that down everywhere but the D.A.'s office. Can't ask for everything."

Clapp had begun scribbling notes. "And that woman Papago lives with might know something. Nell something or other—not Papago, I'm sure of that. And we'll tie a man onto Vespasian, just to be safe. I didn't know you knew him." He dialed the laboratory and gave orders.

"I didn't know *you* knew him."

"Not personally, Max. Vespasian's been around town since '39 or '40, I think. Richards—Vice Detail—has mentioned him. He passes tips to Richards every now and then. Anything for a buck."

"It beats working."

"That's what the bright boys tell me." Clapp considered the unburning bowl of his pipe and then knocked it empty against the side of his battered wooden desk. "I just had a bright idea myself. You know how my mind rambles on. But if I were a private cop like you and I had some interest in George Papago and I thought he'd been killed—you know what I'd do? I'd call on a dumb homicide lieutenant, throw him the bait and let him do my work for me." He smiled engagingly at Thursday.

"You're wasting your time with the government, Clapp. You ought to be in private industry."

"Max, you never were in Denver in your life. What's this Vespasian to you, anyway?"

"I'm trying up yoga and he knows every position."

"I never got a straight answer out of you yet." Clapp

frowned, trying to look fatherly. "You know, your troubles are a big heart, a fat head, and a temper. You get impulsive and try to clean things up too fast, something I had knocked out of me before I reached your age. After all, you're no shining knight on a—"

A lab assistant bustled in to pick up the hatbox and carry it away. When he had gone, Thursday chuckled. "I haven't done a thing this morning to earn a lecture except be a good little citizen."

"Maybe." Clapp worked his mouth and grimaced at the taste in it. "I just know when to get suspicious of you, Max. Don't forget I've seen too many of the bright boys try to make a good thing out of a bad thing. Trying to make some calamity pay off, they get out in the woods, get good and lost morally. This business we're in is pretty inviting that way sometimes. But the complications can drag you into a whole circusful of mischief—if you let them. It's always up to you, of course."

"Don't worry," Thursday said. "I try not to get that cute."

Clapp hit his shoulder as he got up to lock the door to the hall. "Anyway, I'll keep you up on this hat business. You've worked hard enough for it." He stooped beside the little icebox in the corner. "Now when's the last time you drank a beer?"

"Yesterday afternoon at two-thirty." Thursday grinned crookedly. The beer had been with George Papago. "How's that for a straight answer?"

Chapter 7

TUESDAY, AUGUST 9, 1:30 P.M.

Until something broke in the Papago affair—to which he had secured himself a ringside seat—Thursday didn't know where to start looking for the ten IOUs. Back in his office after lunch he called the Telephone Secretarial Service to find if Irene Whitney had phoned him that morning. She hadn't.

He made a few more calls, to an elderly manicurist, to a used-car salesman who got around, to some others. These most close-mouthed of his contacts he set listening for the name of J. X. O'Connell.

The phone rang back at him about one-thirty. A feminine voice asked if he was Mr. Thursday. The voice was throatier than Irene Whitney's and more nervous. "I wanted to see you, but I—are you alone now, Mr. Thursday?"

"For a while. Who is this speaking?"

"I'm phoning from the lobby. If I come right up, may I talk to you?"

"Fourth floor. To the right." When she had hung up, Thursday hastily dialed the cigarstand in the lobby. "Fred? There should be a female just coming out of the phone booths or waiting for an elevator. See her?"

Fred said, "You bet," and whistled softly.

"She alone?"

"Right now, yes. But ask her if she's got a friend, huh?"

"If she had a friend she wouldn't be coming here." Thursday hung up and put on his coat. When a trim, auburn-haired girl timidly pushed open the glass door, he laid down his handful of old letters and went to meet her, smiling courteously.

Fred had put across the right idea. The cut of her green suit meant money and the young body it complimented was worth dressing well. Her wide uncertain eyes picked up copper tints from her hair but the rest of her pale pure face was spiritually pretty, as if to deny the accidental fire in her gaze. To Thursday, the face looked vaguely familiar.

He took her elbow, found it trembling slightly, and steered her to the good chair. "I'm very glad to be able to help you, Miss..."

"Odler." She whispered it and then repeated it decisively. "Yvonne Odler."

Facing her across the desk, he said, "I thought I recognized you from the society sections. *The* Odler family, then?"

"Yes, Mr. Thursday, I wouldn't ever have come to you—except that I was told you were absolutely trustworthy and—"

"Now who could have told you that?" He said it cordially but she didn't answer. "I suppose the Odlers have informational sources just as I do. Merchant princes, patrons of the arts—seriously, I'm happy to be known in that circle."

"You're not teasing?" she asked earnestly, leaning forward. "I don't know what you'll think after . . . I'm in pretty awful trouble."

"If it's any solace to you, Miss Odler, the trouble's usually not as awful as most people in that chair think it is." Pretending not to watch her too closely, he added quietly, "Start anywhere."

She sank white teeth into her full lower lip and gazed helplessly in his direction but seemed to see someone else. The teeth left a tiny dent when her mouth opened to say, "I'm being blackmailed."

Surprise jerked Thursday's head up. "Who's doing it?"

"I don't know," she spilled out quickly. "All I've ever heard him called is Abe. He's nearly as tall as you, only rather plumpish, not very healthy-looking. He's completely—well, evil." She shuddered.

"What's he selling?"

The girl's face became a private scared mask again. "Can't you—must I tell you that?" Thursday nodded sympathetically but kept silent, letting her talk herself into telling him. "But I'd simply die if anybody found out about it. Yet, I suppose—you won't say anything to *anybody*, will you?"

"Miss Odler, I'm bound by some of the same ethics as your family doctor. A private detective who talked couldn't stay open a week."

She said, "Oh," indecisively. She stared down at her purse and wrinkled her forehead and the red color began to creep up from her throat. Finally, she nodded and murmured something to herself and opened the purse. Her delicate hand shook as it pushed a brown envelope halfway across the desk top.

Thursday opened the envelope, not looking at Yvonne Odler because she didn't want to be looked at. He took out six three-by-five photographs, glossy finish, and one photographic negative the same size. Silently, he inspected each picture. After he had held the negative up to the light, he slid everything back into the envelope and left it in the middle of the desk.

He sat back, stony-faced. When the girl glanced up, her eyes were wet. He asked, "Is that all?"

She didn't raise her burnished head. "No. Five other negatives."

"I mean, are these all the poses?"

"Oh, yes!"

"How'd it happen. Miss Odler? Tell me enough so I can fill in the gaps."

"I can't tell you why—why I did such a crazy thing. I suppose I'm not much good. But I swear I didn't know what I was getting into, really I didn't!" Her head stayed bowed. Her muffled voice sounded ready to go into hysteria.

"Look at me!" Thursday commanded and her flushed face flew up, wondering. He said coldly. "Get this. It's none of my business what your character is like. My job is trouble shooting, not repairing complexes. You don't have to apologize to me for a thing as long as I get paid for my work."

Yvonne Odler straightened her shoulders angrily and her transparent skin began to pale. Thursday grinned as she snapped out of it. She smiled back faintly and nodded her head in a sort of apology. "I forgot myself. Another sign that I'm merely a spoiled brat."

"Let's see if I can't reconstruct your luck for you," Thursday said. "Some time back you went to a party, mostly people you didn't know or didn't know very well. Among them was this Abe fellow. You all had a lot to drink, some of you moved on to a smaller, more select party—maybe you tried a hopped-up cigarette—and you were floating on top of the world. First thing you know, you were playing artist's model just for the gag." He flicked the brown envelope with a fingernail. "The next morning all you had were some foggy memories and a lousy headache. The headache didn't get really bad until Abe showed up—with his pictures. How close did I come?"

Yvonne was wide-eyed. She whispered. "You can't know—how *do* you—"

"Pretty old racket, almost formal by now. When did this happen?"

"Two weeks ago. Two weeks last Saturday."

"And the price?"

"A thousand dollars each. For each negative, I mean."

"You're getting off cheap. For an Odler, I'd say that five thousand per would be more like it."

"No, you don't understand," she said, tensing again. "My family—I couldn't stand for them to know. I've been paying out of my allowance."

"But now you're out of allowance."

"I have the second thousand ready but, thinking ahead . . . That's why I came here. I've borrowed all I can from my friends. I've sold some clothes, what jewelry I dared to sell. Oh, if daddy ever found out, he'd be furious!"

"So would the police department. Not with you. With Abe and anybody working with him. The cops keep secrets, too, you know. They have some legal rights I don't have—like kicking a blackmailer around until he coughs up film."

As the girl caught on, her eyes began to brim again. But this time she turned her head to one side to touch her eyes with a lacy handkerchief. Then she sat up regally, her red young mouth tragic. "Please, Mr. Thursday. It's bad enough, it's chancy enough, telling you and you're just one person. The thought of other men seeing those pictures—I'd sooner kill myself, believe me."

"I believe you," Thursday said. "I just felt duty bound to inform you that this town does have a police department. Actually—" he rose suddenly and stepped to the bright window. He socked his right fist into his other palm viciously and after a moment turned back to the girl, smiling thinly "—I'd like a crack at Abe and Company."

"Thank you," Yvonne said huskily. Impetuously, she came around the desk and clasped his big hand, it was still a fist, between her two small ones. "Oh, thank you! You can't know what this means to me."

"Uh-huh," agreed Thursday. "How does Abe contact you?"

"Tomorrow—tomorrow afternoon he said he'd come again. He usually comes about three. I thought if you could come a little earlier, then you could surprise him there. If he carries the negatives with him—"

"That's too much to hope for. I'll be there."

"I'm in the book. Sixth Avenue near Laurel." She paused uncertainly. "We haven't said anything about money, have we?"

"My fee is twenty-five dollars per day plus any unusual expenses. But I never take a fee in advance. I'll bill you afterwards, Miss Odler."

"Oh." She had her checkbook half out of her purse. "Well, if you prefer—but I'm perfectly willing."

Thursday said, "I'll see you tomorrow then—a little before three."

The girl hesitated again, her eyes nervously remembering the brown envelope on his desk. "The pictures—I suppose it's safest to leave them here with you, isn't it?"

"Whatever you think."

"Oh, no! I didn't mean to distrust you but—Mr. Thursday, lock them up somewhere, won't you? I couldn't stand the thought of . . ."

Thursday took up the envelope, crossed to the green metal filing cabinet and slipped the envelope into the top drawer.

While Yvonne watched anxiously, he locked the case and raised his eyebrows at her. "Satisfied?"

"Completely." She held out a warm hand and smiled a little. She said goodbye, that she'd see him tomorrow. Thursday watched her figure walk off down the hall on silken legs and he shook his head with guilty annoyance. Abe's pictures were insidious.

He shut his office door and locked himself in. Then he ambled back to the filing cabinet, got out his keyes and unlocked it. For a long time, he leaned his elbows on its cold top, turning Yvonne Odler's brown envelope over in his hands. A sardonic smile had just begun to twist his mouth when the phone startled the quiet office.

Thursday answered it and Austin Clapp rumbled, "Hi. We just caught up with George Papago."

CHAPTER 8

TUESDAY, AUGUST 9, 2:30 P.M.

Detective Jim Crane, driving the unmarked police sedan, looked the coolest of the three men despite his well-worn black suit. His narrow, stooped shoulders moved effortlessly with the wheel, and his hair gleamed over his reddish, lined face like a snowcap. He hummed while beside him Lieutenant Clapp sweated and growled about needing some sleep.

Sprawled listlessly across the back seat, Max Thursday watched the boring scenery sail by, the sagebrush hills along the University Avenue extension. This back road led eventually to La Mesa, a foothills community ten miles east of San Diego.

Clapp said needlessly, "Right up ahead there, Jim," and

Crane turned off under an arched rustic sign and rolled up a short gravel road that widened into a parking lot. The twig sign letters spelled out MOLYNEUX ALLIGATOR FARM.

A motorcycle policeman roared off about his business as they slid in beside two black-and-white prowl cars. Bryan, a burly patrolman, got up off a running board and crunched toward them. "Lieutenant," he said in greeting and nodded to Crane and Thursday.

"I hear we got a customer," Clapp said.

Bryan jerked his head at the larger of two brown stucco imitations of haciendas that squatted by the parking lot. "That door by the postcard rack and the soda-pop machine. It takes you through the administration building and on out back. He's back there on the path. The doc's there already." He watched the three men trudge on, then sat down again on the running board and wiped out the sweatband of his khaki cap.

Thursday stopped to look at the twelve-foot alligator hide nailed above the doorway and then followed the other two into the administration building where it was cooler. Another door, with turnstile, opened at the rear and beside this was a ticket window, unattended. Sunk in the center of the broad concrete floor, under the skylight, were a pair of pens containing pools and sandy beaches. "The come-on," guessed Clapp, motioning toward the yellow-striped baby alligators. "Step outside for the big show."

As the three detectives walked by, some of the foot-long alligator pups set up a yapping noise and floundered into the water. Thursday nudged Crane and pointed at a glass display case of alligator wallets, belts, purses, and watch straps. "From the cradle to the grave."

"Probably buy them ready-made," Crane said. "Ever try to skin an alligator?"

"No. And don't tell me you have."

The place was deserted. Clapp was already shoving his way through the reluctant turnstile. Fifty yards down the path that rambled through the walled grounds, Thursday could see a knot of men, some uniformed.

The outdoor pools were giant replicas of the pup pens in the administration building. A hundred feet in diameter, they ranged on each side of the path, walled waist-high in brown adobe. Half of each closure was a shallow pond; big boulders and tropical shrubs studded the beach half. In every pen a dozen heavy-trunked alligators lay on the beaches or submerged in the placid water. Their gross armored bodies sunned with no sign of breathing, like fallen statues, while their long jagged mouths grinned perpetual grins. Only the faint trails in the sand showed they were capable of movement.

"The babies had stripes." Crane frowned about it.

"Maybe they outgrew them," Thursday said. "You don't wear yours, Sergeant."

The knot of men opened to absorb the three newcomers. Stein, kneeling, grimaced up at them from beside the sprawled figure at his knees. The medical examiner was a small birdlike man with a dark intent face. "If you'd taken much longer," he welcomed Clapp. "I'd have had this thing solved for you. Jim. Thursday."

"That'll be the day." Clapp knelt briskly beside Stein and then hesitated, scowling painfully at the face-down dead man. Thursday knew the feeling, a sort of angry nausea. Clapp took hold of the head and shifted it on the folded towel so he could see the face. A moment's study and he twisted it back to its former position. He got up slowly and said, "Papago, all right," to Thursday.

It was George Papago but he bore little resemblance to the cocky elaborate dresser who had tricked Thursday the afternoon before. His body was completely nude. The exposed flesh was milk-white in contrast to the black hair. The slightly darker skin of his neck and hands, which had been olive yesterday, was now a pasty gray. The entire body looked boneless, shamefully helpless. The back of the head was matted with hair and a blackish crust.

Clapp broke his own silence. "Jim, better get on the phone and check his home right away." Crane left and the homicide chief looked at the cameraman who nodded. The print man spoke up, "Got the victim's. No surfaces worth playing with. Not in there." He gestured at the nearest alligator enclosure. Clapp glanced around the group and asked, "Find his clothes?"

A patrol car man said, "Searched the road a mile either way, both sides. Nothing, Lieutenant."

"Who found him? When and where?" Clapp's steely eyes fastened on the one stranger there, a lanky sunburnt man with a lantern jaw. He wore a checkered cap, white shirt, and riding breeches, and clutched a two-foot length of broomstick in his fist.

"My name's Long, Roy J. Long, Lieutenant," the lanky man drawled as he moved one faltering step nearer. "I'm keeper for these 'gators. I reckon I'm the one to tell you about it."

"Lieutenant Clapp—homicide. You the owner, Mr. Long?"

"No, sir, that's Mr. Molyneux. He isn't here right now. Mrs. Molyneux—his wife—you know she felt kind of sick and he took her up to the house to lie down." He stabbed his piece of broomstick toward the stucco structure beside the administration building. "They live in there. I can go get them if you—"

"Never mind, thanks. I can hear your story and then we'd like formal statements from all you people later on."

"I found him—whoever he is—I guess about an hour ago. He was in one of the pens. In with Prettyboy—the pen right there."

"An hour ago?" Clapp turned to Stein who was brushing off his knees. "He was killed last night, wasn't he?"

The medical examiner straightened, surprised. "You're getting on to my racket. My rough estimate was going to be fourteen to eighteen hours ago."

"Sapped?"

"Not exactly. At the moment I'd say a billy, lead pipe, jack handle, something like that. Not a blackjack. I'm pretty certain skull crushed by blunt instrument is cause of death. No other marks on him except some scratches on the left calf, both sides."

The cameraman cleared his throat. "Lieutenant, there's little or no blood on the sand over there where they said they found him. It looks like he got it somewhere else and somebody dumped him over there after the blood had stopped flowing."

"There's *some* grit in the coagulation," Stein protested hotly. "The blood hadn't *completely* coagulated when the wound came into contact with the sand."

"Thanks, both of you," said Clapp and swung back to Roy Long. "It appears that the dead man has been here since last night, Mr. Long. How come you didn't notice him till an hour ago?"

Long smiled weakly. "That's what I was going to say, Lieutenant. He wasn't out in plain sight. Over behind some of the rocks." He pointed past the alligators in the pen at an open den of boulders at the far side. "I still wouldn't have found him except some fool sightseer stood up on the wall to take a picture and made some crack about how it took a lot of guts to sun-bathe in with the crocodiles. The fool called them crocs. I hopped over to see and then—" He shrugged, glancing involuntarily at the body.

Clapp sent a patrolman after a blanket to cover the body. Then he put Long through the story again. Then he had Long lead him around to where they could look over the wall and see where the body was found. One of the prowl cars left on a call and a moment later Clapp dismissed the other one.

Thursday had spent his time leaning against the wall listening but not butting into the homicide chief's routine. After another check with the camera and print men, Clapp sauntered over to lean beside him. Silently, the two looked at the somnolent alligators.

Clapp said, "Well, there passes one bright boy, Papago."

"Yeah. I've seen him around, could take him or leave him alone. Still makes you mad, whoever it is."

"I suppose he mixed in something too tricky, too cute even for him. This place is closed at night, all sound sleepers. From those couple of flakes of blood on the sand, I'd say he was dumped over the wall down here in plain sight and the alligators dragged him back of the rocks. Nasty thing to think about."

"Any sign of the car that brought him?"

"No. You saw the road outside. First of all, it's gravel, and second, it's been driven over all day."

"You can't have everything. Think of the glory you'll get out of this one."

Clapp laughed hollowly. "I'd trade that for a little rest." He squinted his eyes in the glare.

Stein said, behind them, "You going to want anything else, Clapp, or can we get out of this sun?"

"Sorry," Clapp said, turning around. "Take him away any time. Stein, can I have the preliminary autopsy report by after dinner?"

"Well, slave driver, seeing that you asked so politely . . ." The medical examiner waved a goodbye and walked down the path, whistling.

"The point that bothers me," Thursday said, gazing at the blanketed shape still on the path, "is why? Why cart him in here, taking the chance of waking up the Molyneux family or Long, when there are so many deserted canyons handy?"

"Why not? Dandy place to lose a body—toss it in with a pack of hungry alligators—" Clapp broke off. "Yeah, I see what you mean. Nothing happened to the body, did it?"

"Maybe the killer figured the same way you did. If it worked it would beat our pal the ocean all hollow. It'd beat any method of body disposal except flushing it down the john."

Roy Long was lingering near them, just out of earshot,

uncertain that he had been dismissed. He came forward eagerly when Clapp motioned to him. "Anything I can do, Lieutenant?"

"I thought these lizards ate meat."

"Reckon they do. Oh—I see." He grinned. "That's right, we feed them raw meat. First-rate horse meat and liver. We buy it right over there in La Mesa, and just the best since 'gators can be mighty finicky. But they only eat every two weeks and I fed them all yesterday. They wouldn't touch a bite today if I served them on a silver platter."

Clapp asked, "Are they too finicky for human meat? I always thought these things were man-eaters."

"Not a chance!" Long drawled. "Maybe out in the swamps, if you riled one up, you might have trouble. But these 'gators are peace-loving creatures and most of them hatched right here. Only takes them ten years to reach full growth, you know."

Stubbornly, Clapp persisted. "They handled the body, scratched up his leg with their teeth."

"Only out of curiosity, Lieutenant. Lookee here." Long vaulted over the wall and tromped up to an alligator fifteen feet long. "This is Prettyboy," he called to his audience. "He's one that was born in the swamps and never got caged until he'd reached eight feet. Watch him."

Clapp muttered, "I suppose he knows his business."

"I'm not going in after him," Thursday whispered back.

Long rattled his piece of broomstick along Prettyboy's serrated back. A second later the alligator's big golden eye winked open. Long tapped the reptile's snout and backed away across the sand, stepping over sleeping bulks as he bumped into them. By the time he reached the wall, Prettyboy had gotten the idea. He hoisted his ponderous leathery body on spindly legs and trotted after the keeper. He moved at a pace that surprised Clapp and Thursday, grating his belly over the backs of other alligators until he'd reached Long's feet. There he planted his snout across the keeper's boot toes and lay down, eyes again closed.

Long grinned, disengaged his feet and leaped back over the wall. "See?" he said proudly. "I'd bet my savings they wouldn't nibble a man, dead or alive, unless I starved them a month or two. That trick I just pulled—you ought to see the tourists go for it."

As if in agreement, Prettyboy opened his jaws nearly to his eye sockets, showing off a pink cavern rimmed with pointed teeth. He roared lustily, a booming note like a bass steam whistle.

"Smartest bull I ever seen," Long said when he could be heard.

"You bet." Thursday smiled at Clapp who was twisting a forefinger in one ear. "Well, Clapp, your killer doesn't know any more about alligators than we do. That narrows the field down a lot."

"Oh, sure. Like finding out he had two eyes. Come on—let's go back to that office. I feel a headache coming on."

"The sun or the case?"

"Two guesses."

Going up the path, they were hailed by Jim Crane. "Just heard, Austin. The D.A.'s on his way out."

"Fine medicine," Clapp said sourly.

CHAPTER 9

TUESDAY, AUGUST 9, 3:30 P.M.

They heard the ambulance arrive out front as they strolled toward the rear ticket entrance of the administration building. Crane was ticking off items on his fingers. "I broke it to Papago's woman, this Nell Kopke, but she didn't have anything to add. Papago went out yesterday afternoon and just never came home. She still doesn't know where, she says."

"Any visitors or phone calls before hand?" Clapp asked.

Thursday looked away, toward the stretcher bearers advancing down the path, his hands chilled by a fleeting premonition. But he heard Crane's voice say. "No," and his shoulders relaxed a trifle. The white-haired detective added, "I doubt if she'll ever let on, anyway, not to us. She isn't putting herself out any to be nice. Not to a cop."

"We'll try gentling her later," said Clapp. "Meantime I want you to pull in this fellow Vespasian I told you about—Max, you got his address handy?" Thursday rattled it off. "He's just a cheap chiseler—scare him all you want. But get that silly story of his a dozen times over, now that it means what it does."

Crane nodded. "I'll grab a ride in with Stein. And Papago." He went on out the front door to the ambulance, leaving Clapp and Thursday alone in the administration building. The alligator pups began barking and floundering once more.

Clapp tried to cheer himself up. "Maybe this thing isn't as goofed up as it looks. Suppose your Vespasian and Papago's woman were two-timing George and he caught on. Or for that matter—"

"I don't know about that," Thursday said slowly. He felt responsible for dragging Vespasian this close to the fire. Still . . . he sensed that the fortuneteller was implicated to some unknown degree. "I just don't think that little operator could hit as hard as Papago was hit."

"Maybe not. But I've seen that woman and she could. She's the athletic type. Besides, any weakling can do wonders with a lead pipe."

"Too simple for this case. Papago might have welshed on a bet or tried to foreclose some old IOUs. Or something."

"If it had been gambling trouble, we'd have found him in that canyon you mentioned. But you're right in a way, Max. Just not my luck to draw down a simple one—especially with you around."

"Benedict losing his prize fish a week before the trial—*he'll* go for the gambling angle. I'll give you five to one on that, as long as you don't mention I think so, too."

"Speak of the devil," murmured Clapp. Thursday looked out the door. The police ambulance was just rolling out the gravel driveway as a dark-green Cadillac sedan turned in. The Cadillac parked next to Clapp's car and two men got out. "No bet," Clapp added and went to the door to wave a hand at Leslie Benedict.

The district attorney of San Diego marched up to the administration building as if on parade. He never meant to act officious for he was too precise a man to show off, but the bearing of his lean erect body always seemed too correct to be true. He had only just passed forty and he was not an ugly man. But the smooth regularity of his deeply tanned, short-mouthed face gave him the cool appearance of an egg. In all published photographs he wore a hat to break this symmetry, the only political trick Benedict ever stooped to. The press of his blue suit, the knot of his tie, the high gloss of his shoes . . . as always. Thursday felt unshaven and sloppy next to Leslie Benedict.

Ed Wales, the one-man brigade Benedict led, tried to be like him. He was a big young man, a bright young man with rimless spectacles and an insincere smile.

Clapp said to Thursday, "Favor to me, Max—go send Long in here, will you?"

Thursday grinned, understanding, and pushed through the turnstile with no more than one chilly glance from Benedict's yellowish eyes. He sent Roy Long in to Clapp and loafed around on the path, smoking a cigarette. Clapp was right, he reflected. No use hanging around as if he were eavesdropping on official business. On the other hand, he didn't want to skulk out here in the sun and give Benedict the idea he was afraid of him. After five minutes of consideration, Thursday decided to rejoin the forces of law but keep his mouth discreetly shut.

"By tomorrow morning I'd like to read over the statements of everyone on these premises." Benedict was telling Clapp. "The owners and Mr. Long, and I understand there are some Mexicans who work here during the day, also."

"I gave them a half a day off when this trouble came up," Long drawled. "I reckoned we'd be shut down for the afternoon, at least. But those boys didn't see anything or they'd have put up a holler."

Ed Wales sidled up to Thursday. "Hello, Max," he said, voice muted so as not to bother his superior. "What are you doing out here?"

"I've been expecting that question from your boss, too."

Wales shook his head, deeply worried. He whispered, "He doesn't show it, of course, but he's upset. You can't blame him, losing Papago just on the eve, as it were. I imagine somebody didn't want Papago to come to trial."

"That what Benedict figures, too, Ed?"

"What's more likely?"

Thursday didn't answer.

Benedict swung his impersonal gaze around the group. "Let me sum up," he said didactically. "George Papago was murdered between nine o'clock last night and one o'clock this morning by person or persons unknown. Place unknown. Murder weapon unknown but presumed to be a bludgeon of some sort. The victim's clothes and personal articles were stolen or destroyed. Papago's body was placed in one of the alligator pens in the hope that the reptiles would consume it and destroy all traces of the crime. Have I stated the fact correctly?"

Then Thursday said, "No," flatly.

It had slipped out but when he saw the shocked look on Wales's face, he knew he was going to defend his hunch. Benedict didn't register any emotion, but behind his back Clapp grimaced.

Thursday said, "The killer didn't expect the alligators to

gollup down Papago. Maybe he wanted it to look that way but that wasn't the main reason. What he really wanted was to make sure Papago's death got a good spread, a big splash."

Now Clapp looked interested. "You mean as a warning to somebody. Who?"

"I don't know. But I do know this—tomorrow there won't be a newspaper reader in Southern California who won't know about Papago. Just because of the alligator angle."

Clapp chewed his lip, thinking that one over. But Benedict, whose eyes had not left Thursday's since the blunt interruption, spoke deliberately. "That idea's certainly worth consideration, Thursday. I'm glad you happen to be here as an expert on the press and their sensational handling of crime news." Thursday smiled back at him wryly, knowing what would come next. "And that brings up a point which I had refrained from mentioning. How *do* you happen to be here?"

"He came out with me," Clapp said. "Max turned up a piece of this case. That Vespasian. Naturally, he's interested."

"Indeed? But I can't understand his position in an official investigation. In fact, Lieutenant, I've never been able to understand Thursday's semi-official standing with your department, particularly in view of his record and his methods."

Clapp's heavy face reddened and he jammed his hands in his pockets. "Mr. Benedict, I run my outfit my way. Knowing Max, I take a slightly different view of said record and methods, and that doesn't mean I condone anything, either. So if you want to file a complaint. I'm sure my chief will read it."

"Not at all," Leslie Benedict said decisively. "I'm expressing the opinion of my office, but only to you since I see no cause yet for formal complaint. However, I will add this—" he took a half-turn toward Thursday "—I don't intend to abide your interference in *my* work, Thursday. If necessary, I'll have you detained for obstructing justice. Is my view clear?"

"Les," said Thursday amiably, "you keep up that kind of talk and you're going to antagonize me."

Wales began with, "Now see here," but couldn't think how to finish. Benedict merely let fall, like a theater curtain, a look of cool amusement across his face.

A car squealed to a halt on the gravel outside. "Reporters," Clapp said. "All in Osborn's car." He added, "Max, would you—"

"Sure." Thursday grinned briefly and went outdoors. He boiled inside because he had acted like a child and Benedict had squelched him like one. He wondered why the D.A. always brought out his impulsive worst. Two entirely different men, yes, but both working to the same end.

The three men and the woman who got out of Osborn's Ford surrounded him with questions. He said, "Don't know from nothing. The big boys will see you in a second." They still wanted to chatter but he shouldered by them and went on out to Clapp's car.

Merle Osborn trailed after him. A tall brusque young woman, she could be handsome when she put forth the effort. Today she wore her usual mannish suit of gray worsted, one button missing, and flat-heeled shoes. During the man shortage, she had been promoted to the police beat, an important post on the lurid *Sentinel*, and she had been good enough to keep it since.

She caught up with Thursday, her bright round eyes looked him up and down, and she said, "Temper, my boy. *You* didn't have a flat coming out here. And those other three lugs were about as much help as—"

Thursday grinned toothily to please her. "I tried to call you after lunch. Ever heard of anybody using the name J. X. O'Connell? Phony lawyer."

"No. I'll listen, though. What's your connection with this present turmoil?"

"Honey, I wish I knew."

"Okay, lie to me."

He poked back into place a strand of brown hair that had slipped out of her severe coiffure. "Now don't act hurt. You know you'll get it first, lies and all."

Merle squeezed his hand unobtrusively. "Your subtle consideration, that's why I can't resist you." He shrugged and she said, "Tomorrow's my night off. Time was I didn't have to remind you."

"I'll be there." Clapp signaled from the doorway and Thursday gave her a little shove. "Now earn your pay." She smiled back at him as she caught up with the other reporters filing into the administration building.

Thursday clambered into the back seat of the police sedan and lit a cigarette. He reviewed his glimpses of the long fuse that had finally exploded into the Papago killing. He wondered how soon he could pass his tiny store of information on to Clapp without jeopardizing his client. He also wondered if Clapp was keeping anything back from him. And finally, he was almost dozing, gazing sleepily at the road that led by the Molyneux Alligator Farm.

A blue Buick convertible slowed and he thought it was going to turn up the driveway. But the driver was merely staring curiously. At what, Thursday couldn't figure. Everybody but him was inside out of sight. Of the three cars on the parking lot—Clapp's, Benedict's, Osborn's—all were unmarked and unnotable.

Yet the driver of the convertible stared as if she already knew this was the scene of murder. Then Thursday sat up hastily as he recognized the woman driver, and, seeing him, Irene Whitney sped her blue convertible swiftly on toward La Mesa.

CHAPTER 10

WEDNESDAY, AUGUST 10, 9:30 A.M.

Nell Kopke sat across the desk from him, one arm around the homely Georgie who played with the zipper on her purse. She wasn't drunk but she had cloves on her breath. The morning light was unkind to her drawn face.

Thursday said, "I know how tough it is on both of you. They'll do all they can."

"But that don't bring George back," she said bitterly. "I guess I surprise you, huh? After being out at the house yesterday, I mean. Well, I loved him, never mind how we talked. We always figured someday—" She broke off to hug the little boy to her roughly. "Now poor Georgie hasn't got any father at all."

Georgie sucked his thumb through the embrace while his great eyes pondered the detective. Thursday rephrased what he had been saying for ten minutes. "Well, I know absolutely they'll find out who did it. I realize how little comfort—"

"Cops!" Her sensual mouth narrowed scornfully. "I don't need their help."

"They'll give it, though. They don't like this, either."

"They don't see the same way I do. I'll take care of this myself. For George's sake. That's the way he'd have wanted it."

"No, it seems to me that George would have liked you to stay out of trouble. Because of the kid."

Nell's dull eyes raked him boldly. "You want me to just sit and chew my tongue, huh?"

He kept from pointing out that Papago wouldn't be in the police morgue now if he had done more of that. He got up from the swivel chair to stretch his legs, wondering if anything valuable was to be gotten from her. Probably not, because the gambler hadn't been killed in connection with his usual business. He felt sure of that and, anyway, Clapp and Benedict would have that obvious channel dragged and dredged.

"I thought so," Nell spoke up accusingly and then went back to brooding. Georgie skipped over to the window to peep at the dizzy distance down. She said, "I didn't tell the cops you were out to the house yesterday, you know."

"I know. Thanks."

"You want to know why?"

"Because you haven't been telling the cops anything." Thursday turned to the wall map behind his desk. It was a huge map of the city, mounted on heavy beaverboard, which was intended to give clients the idea he had the whole town at his fingertips. Just the contrast between this woman and that, like peasant and princess, started his mind working over Irene Whitney. All he knew of his client was her looks and her car. He ran his forefinger from La Mesa on the map down to the alligator farm.

"No, that wasn't why," Nell said shakily. Behind him, he heard her purse zip open and he wondered if she was getting out a handkerchief to cry into. Then her voice went up, "Because I wanted to do this myself!"

He started to turn just as the office rocked with explosion and a small cyclone rushed over his head. Thursday spun around his desk in a crouch and dove into the woman.

Georgie began laughing excitedly at the noise. The impact between Thursday and the woman was solid; Nell was tall and husky. At the instant of collision he noticed she was trembling violently, then he broke away from her with her little revolver safe in his hand.

She didn't try to run. She stood flat-footed, her wide-apart eyes glaring defiantly. Thursday said, "You're going to talk to the cops now, like it or not."

Georgie still laughed and clapped his hands. "Do it again!" he pleaded. "Do it again!"

"You'll never turn me in," Nell said sullenly. "You do and I'll tell what I know."

Thursday smiled bleakly. "Guess again, honey. I'm not behind any eight ball in this business. For professional reasons. I'd just as soon not mix with it, but I didn't kill George. That's the crazy idea you got in mind, isn't it?"

The animal glow began to die in her eyes. Finally, the first doubt flickered across her broad face. "But I thought—"

"I'll tell you something, Nell, you should have learned by now. You're not the kind of woman who ought to think. No, I'm not mad because I know how upset you are. But don't try thinking because you're not good at it."

Somehow, obscurely, that reminded her of her appearance. She straightened her dress over her figure and made certain her long hair was lying properly down her back.

Thursday sighed and went to the window. Below, in front of the Moulton Building, a prowl car had jerked to a stop. "Somebody reported the shot. We're going to have cops."

Nell began to look frightened and he felt sorry for her. She gathered Georgie and her purse, looked around for a closet and didn't see one. "I'll go someplace," she said uncertainly and headed for the door.

Thursday grabbed her arm. "That won't do. That hall will be lined with people looking out doors. Can you keep the kid quiet for five minutes?"

"Sure. You'll keep shut up, won't you, precious—if mommy tells you to?"

"I want to hear the noise again," Georgie said plaintively.

"The desk," Thursday said. He led her and the youngster around behind it. Between the two columns of drawers, the knee space was a small wooden cave, hidden from anyone not sitting in the swivel chair. Thursday had Georgie crawl in first. He knelt and whispered to him, "Now this is a game, kid. You and mommy hide here and don't make any noise at all. You do it right and I'll buy you an ice-cream cone. Okay?"

The youngster looked out at him blankly. Nell repeated the instructions and got into the cramped space beside him. Thursday sat down in his swivel chair and wheeled as close to the desk as he could, until his knees were tight against the woman's warm side. He got a rag out of the bottom drawer. He dumped the cartridges from the cylinder and was making a pretense of cleaning the gun when a hand tried the door.

The prowl car man was named Hoover, and Thursday knew him from a shoplifting case two months before. Hoover said, "Hi, sorry to—" He broke off and came all the way in, shutting out the buzz in the hall. "Maybe we found it, huh?"

"How are you, Hoover?" Thursday said and grinned foolishly. "I just pulled a dumb-fool stunt. I was hoping nobody noticed."

"Noticed!" Hoover snorted and came over to look at the short blue-steel Colt. "Report we got was that a bomb went off. Cleaning accident?"

"Yeah. Overlooked one that nearly took my head off."

"Where'd it go?"

Thursday got up and showed him on the map. In the green square that represented Balboa Park, there was a small hole drilled into the beaverboard.

For a second, Hoover looked interested enough to come behind the desk and inspect the bullet hole which almost blended into the map. But he got out his report book instead. He wrote a few lines, then glanced up, pencil poised. "Got a permit for that .32, haven't you, Thursday? Not that you're carrying it this minute but..."

"Sure," Thursday lied. "I may be dumb enough to part my hair with the thing but I'm not that dumb."

Hoover put his book away and grinned. "Well, consider yourself warned. Hope you're still alive next time I see you."

After he had gone, Thursday waited a full minute before he told the pair under the desk it was safe. Georgie wriggled free first. "I want a double-decker, chocolate and strawberry. That costs a dime."

Thursday gave him a dime.

"I did good, didn't I? I wanted to sneeze but I didn't." He laboriously buttoned the coin into his pocket and ran back to the window.

Thursday said, "I wonder how good I did." He regarded Nell who was again smoothing her dress over the fullness of her body. She stopped in the process, gave him an obstinate look and continued preening. He said, "Maybe I should have let the cops have you."

"All right, so I owe you something."

"What gave you the idea I killed George?"

"You killed some other people once."

"Most people don't remember two years back."

"George told me."

"Well, don't let people put ideas in your head. The cops don't think your own alibi for Monday night is very hot."

"You know that's not true." Nell said stubbornly. "I went over to some friends and we played pinochle. The cops say they won't bother me any more."

"I was just asking. Oh, well." Thursday sat down and extended his legs under the desk luxuriously. "Nell, I didn't kill George. I didn't have a thing against him and I don't know who did. I'm working on the same business George was when it happened. So I may find out, especially if I can get a little co-operation from you. That includes not taking potshots at me."

"You don't know how lucky you really are. I'm a terrific shot as a rule. That gun must be off or something."

She seemed to take some sort of simple pride in her shooting which was as awkward as her thinking. Thursday reflected that she probably regarded herself as quite a brain. He said. "How about it? Do we co-operate and help George together?"

"Okay, I guess so," Nell said slowly. "Just what is it you want me to do, huh?"

"The first thing is not to excite the cops. You're more important out of jail than in." Thursday reeled off the flattery, ready to say anything that would keep her out of his hair. "The best thing would be to stay home and think. Think of everything George said and did in the last few days. Whatever seems not quite right, why, you call me up and tell me. I'll keep a record up here and pretty soon we may stumble onto something. It's because you're valuable that way that I didn't throw you to the cops."

"Oh," she said and looked surprised. "Can I have my gun back? George gave it to me."

"All right," Thursday said. He handed her the .32 and then its ammunition, just in case. But Nell dropped the Colt in her purse without reloading, called Georgie and took his hand.

"I'll call you as soon as I think of something," she promised. From the door she asked, "Was that really why you didn't turn me in?"

"What else?"

"I figured it was so you could make a pass at me." Mother and child departed, leaving Max Thursday a whole new line of thought.

CHAPTER 11

WEDNESDAY, AUGUST 10, 10:30 A.M.

Clapp wasn't around headquarters when Thursday phoned so he thumbed to the L section of the directory and made some checkup calls. Then he drove down Broadway to the waterfront and around the curve of the harbor to the Westgate Sea Products Company.

Here, in the tuna cannery, he ran down Rosa Lalli. She existed, which seemed to bear out Vespasian's tale of that corner of his career. She was a dark buxom girl, with a pretty sheeplike face, whom a foreman brought up from the packing belt. Thursday asked a few vague questions regarding a mythical insurance claim and departed without worrying anybody. His estimate amused him: that the ubiquitous gallant, Vespasian, was about as high as his light-of-love's chin.

Going round by the foot of Market Street, he spotted Clapp's broad back turning into the tiny corner cafe opposite the police station.

"Not much new," Clapp admitted when Thursday slid onto the stool next to him. "Traffic bunch picked up Papago's car this morning a couple blocks from the post office. Overparking. There's some blood dried onto the right-hand side of the front seat so that's evidently where the Greek got his."

"You think the killer carted Papago out to the alligator farm in his own car and then brought it back?"

"Good a way to figure as any."

"Prints?"

Clapp grunted. "You know better than that. Fingerprints have been publicized so much, it's the first thing your average murderer thinks about."

"That's a neat concept, Clapp, the average murderer. You're getting bitter."

"Well, this coffee doesn't help much." Clapp made a nauseated face at his cup. "Personally, I'm thanking my lucky stars for that carhop knifing night before last. Makes us look good and gives the papers something juicy to chew on. That way they don't ride us so much." He snickered disgustedly. "Boy, how's that for ill winds!"

"You're forgiven. What about Papago's clothes?"

"Nothing yet, maybe never. But, unless it's something exceptional, clothes are mainly identification and we don't need that here. We all know it's Papago."

"Well . . . maybe it was having to get rid of the clothes that gave the killer the idea of making a warning out of Papago's body."

"Name it and you can have it."

Thursday's own coffee came. He sipped it and shuddered. "I remember reading about a case up in San Berdoo a few years back. Victim's clothes were destroyed, not because of identification, but to cover up. The killer wanted to get rid of a wallet and he figured if all the clothes were missing nobody'd think about the wallet—or what might be in it."

"I don't remember this one. Did they?"

"No. It came out later, after they'd caught their man. This wallet—" Thursday heard the limb creak as he climbed farther out on it "—contained a calling card, presence of same being known to the victim's wife. The name on it was a phony but the printing could have been traced."

"Printers don't keep much record of little jobs like calling cards," Clapp objected. "Of course, if the phony had distinguished himself at the time of purchase, like an argument over price or something..."

"Well, the card was important to the killer for some reason like that. The point is that the card's absence from the wallet might have been noticed. But what did the card matter when everything was missing?"

"Um," said Clapp. "More coffee?"

"This is more than enough. Well, I just thought I'd mention it."

Clapp wasn't too interested. He said instead, "I been out with Jim and a pair of the boys, trying to get a line on what Papago was up to Monday night. Ever spend your mornings in bars? You sure meet some droll customers."

"Dig up anything?"

"Clocked Papago's final rounds practically to the minute." Clapp shook his head. "What a capacity that Greek had! Eleven different saloons sold him a drink or two."

"He sounds more like a gypsy. What does anybody do in eleven different bars?"

"From the way it sounds, he was dodging somebody."

In the cup Thursday held, the coffee sloshed slightly. Then he drained the black acid and set it down. "Know who?"

"Yes and no. Come on, let's make a break for it." Clapp paid both checks, brushed aside Thursday's dime and lumbered out into the sunlight. The two big men teetered on the curb, the Market Street traffic rushing by.

Thursday waited for Clapp to speak. When it appeared that the homicide chief was going to continue frowning at the hot asphalt, he prompted, "Are you going to tell me or aren't you?"

"Oh, yeah." Clapp had been off somewhere else. "There's this nice little bar near the Frémont. McCloskey's Shining Hour. That's where Papago ended up before his date with the alligators. He was sitting there at one of the tables having a drink with a gray-haired fellow when the guy who had been chasing him came along."

"And?"

"The stranger—call him the killer if you want—took Papago away with him. The gray-haired chap went out about the same time." Clapp dusted his hands together. "Scratch Papago."

Thursday said, "You got witnesses for all this, Clapp?"

Clapp snorted. "You think I'm making it up? Sure, I got witnesses. Plenty. They're vague as usual on some of the details—time and so on—but their stories'll hold up. If and when."

"How about the gray-haired man?"

"Got a fair description of him. Tall, good clothes, mustache, stick, man-of-distinction stuff. We'll publicize it, get him to come in. A little luck and he'll be able to put the finger right on the killer for us."

Thursday knew the crazy answer but he put the question anyway. "And how about this mysterious stranger who chased Papago around town and took him away? What's he look like?"

"Not too much to go on there. McCloskey's barkeep knew the gray-haired man by sight and Papago from the papers lately. But the stranger was a new man. Tall and thin and dark. That'll fit a lot of men."

"Even me," Thursday agreed.

"Well, if I thought you were wasting your youth in bars . . ."

said Clapp, mock-serious. "At any rate, this raises the stock of your friend Vespasian quite a bit. He may be a latter-day alchemist but I don't think he could stretch out to that description. Happy?" He started across the street.

Thursday waved so-long and called, "Frankly, I got better men to worry about than that sneaker." First on his list was himself.

CHAPTER 12

WEDNESDAY, AUGUST 10, 2:30 P.M.

After a grouchy lunch in a rear booth at the Saddlerock Grill, he kicked around his office for a while, brooding over the fallibility of witnesses and mankind in general. He was not surprised to be remembered by the bartenders. But he hadn't counted on being tabbed as the man who had taken George Papago away. By sheer human vagary, the shadowy O'Connell had gotten safely lost somewhere in the middle.

There was one grimly cheering aspect to his entire future: this afternoon he hoped to close with somebody tangible at Yvonne Odler's place. Thursday cracked his knuckles in anticipation.

At two-thirty precisely he parked his gray Oldsmobile alongside the sunny lawns of Balboa Park and strode across Sixth Avenue. The Devonshire was a late California building of stucco and glazed tile and glass brick. U-shaped around an orderly jungle of patio. All apartments on both stories opened onto the patio.

Thursday ran down the names by the mailboxes, found ODLER listed as 2A, went up to the encircling balcony and knocked on her door.

"Mr. Thursday, I'm glad you're early. I've been worrying about—you know." He smiled back at her warm just-woke-up smile that seemed to establish a bond between them. The rest of Yvonne was all white flesh and copper. There were coppery tones in her hair and lashes and sandals and in the stark sheath of metallic negligee that dove deep beneath her firm breasts.

Thursday said, "Don't worry," and stepped into her deep carpet. A record player was making languid music. Yvonne took his hat and bumped the door shut with her shoulder, and he followed her cloud of perfume across the living room.

The room was big and bright-walled, an odd background for the girl's face which belonged in a church choir. The furniture was built in outlandish angular shapes as if the designer was jaded with the ordinariness of life. The paintings were abstracts in shouting purples and yellows and greens. Queer twisted statuettes guarded each end of the too-wide divan. The trapezoid block that represented a coffee table bore a lavish tray of salty-looking hors d'oeuvres and a long-necked bottle of yellow chartreuse.

"Please," Yvonne murmured, offering him the room. She sat down in the middle of the divan, had a blushing accident with the slit hem of her negligee, and opened the bottle. "I thought I'd make your visit as pleasant as possible, Mr. . . . well, since you've caught me deshabille, I'd might as well call you Max, hadn't I? Or don't you ever mix business and pleasure, Max?"

"My business is my pleasure, Miss Odler."

"How courtly! And something to drink to." She leaned forward to fill the two cordial glasses and Thursday kept an eye on her bent head as he transferred his fountain pen from his shirt to his right-hand coat pocket.

Yvonne rose with the two brimming yellow glasses. "Guaranteed to make you forget the weather," she said softly.

Thursday turned his back on her and walked over to attach the night chain on the door. He heard Yvonne sigh, "Why, Max . . ."

He returned to her and took one of the glasses. She tilted her face to look up at him. She whispered, "Please take me seriously. I've remembered nothing but you since yesterday. You weren't what I expected." Her eyes got wider as she drifted closer until their bodies were touching gently.

"Thank you," Thursday said. He put an arm around her neck and poured his glass of chartreuse down her back.

Yvonne sprang away, horrified. Her own drink tumbled on the carpet and she clutched behind herself. "Max! Why did you do that?"

Thursday put his hand in his coat pocket and shoved the barrel of the fountain pen forward against the lining. He grinned maliciously. "I don't drink."

As she retreated before him, the spiritual look ebbed from her face until she was a hot-eyed young imp. Her new hateful face couldn't believe the shape of his coat pocket.

Thursday said, "If you think it's my fountain pen, take a chance. Go ahead and try to warn him."

She licked her lips and said weakly, "I don't know what you're talking about."

"Sure not." He caught up with her behind the divan, spun her around and jabbed her sticky back with the concealed pen. "Avaunt, honey. And be a mighty good girl."

She began a protest but he jabbed her again and she submitted. They opened a door into a dim hallway with three more doors. The kitchen was empty and so was the bathroom. At the third door, Yvonne tried to turn around but Thursday opened the door himself and kneed her roughly into the bedroom.

Most of the room was a low cushiony bed. The decor was even more pagan than the living room, and mirrored. Beside the dressing table, a tall man in shirtsleeves was taking a swig from a pint whisky bottle.

It wasn't J. X. O'Connell; Thursday felt a twinge of disappointment at that. The stranger was tall enough but he was a puffy young man with mousy hair and big ears. His straw hat and plaid coat were thrown carelessly across the bed beside the black case of a Speed Graphic camera.

He and Thursday looked at each other silently for a moment. His Adam's apple moved twice before any words came out and then his voice was cracked. "What are you doing here?"

Yvonne dodged away from Thursday but not between the two men. "Abe! He's come back the way I said he would! Don't let him touch me, please!"

Abe blinked from Yvonne to the implacable Thursday and tried to look mean. "Kind of caught you red-handed this time, didn't I, mister? You think I'm going to stand for you annoying my wife the way you've—"

"Shut up," Thursday advised.

Abe closed his mouth and eyed the girl helplessly. Thursday sat down on the bed and took his hand out of his pocket since Abe wasn't going to be much to handle. He told Abe, "Now let's face facts, not play house. You're lucky you're not married to this tramp. You're that lucky, anyway."

Yvonne spat out a phrase.

"Now you're talking to me like you mean it." Thursday picked up the Speed Graphic. The metal tag riveted to the case read *Property of Don Kerner Photo Studio.*

"I just rented the camera there," Abe said quickly. "I was going to take some pictures this afternoon in the park."

Thursday laughed appreciatively. Then he ducked. He snaked out an arm in time to block the hand mirror Yvonne intended to axe him with. He knocked the mirror from her hand and held her easily at arm's length while she kicked and swore at him until she was tired.

"Back to the living room," Thursday ordered. "I don't like these parties where the guests wind up in the bedroom."

He herded them out to the divan and sat them down. He pulled up a weird chair and faced them across the coffee table. "Let's have a drink," he suggested.

Some hope came into Yvonne's eyes and she smiled tentatively. "That's the first truly sensible thing you've said."

"Not me, Yvonne. Just you and Abe." He chuckled. "I've sworn off, didn't I tell you? Particularly off mickeys."

"Please let me tell you, Max," Yvonne begged. She leaned forward earnestly, careless of her negligee again, and her lower lip quivered. "I know I have no right to the sympathy of a decent person. But, Max, he made me do it! He forced me! He threatened me with all sorts of terrible things if I didn't help him."

Thursday asked Abe, "How does it feel to be thrown to the wolves?"

Yvonne slipped down to the carpet on her knees and began crying. "Don't you believe me? I need your help—oh, so desperately, Max! Get me away from these people, oh, please!"

"You'll never need anybody's help—not with an act like that. Now drink your drink and let's get chummy." He collected the two glasses and filled them while Yvonne cursed him without a break or repetition for a full thirty seconds. Then he said calmly, "The drink."

She got back up on the divan defiantly and downed the glass of chartreuse. One glance from Thursday and the flabby photographer followed suit. Thursday said, "This is shaping up rough for you two. Especially you, Abe—you don't have the Odler connections."

"I don't know a thing you mean," Abe muttered.

"Are you dumber than I think you are? You just heard her try to make you the fall guy. That's just a sample of what lies ahead. Of course, you know how to make it easier on yourself."

There was an instant of silence while Abe sneaked a look sideways at the girl. She said viciously, "You listen to him, fat boy, and you know what'll happen to you."

Abe's mouth worked. "I don't know a thing you mean," he repeated to Thursday.

Thursday shrugged and refilled their glasses and made them drink again. He said, "Then let me tell you. Yvonne's tale of woe yesterday stuck in my throat. Kind of coincidental that two similarly persecuted women should decide to talk up to the same private cop. I was expecting this layout this afternoon. I didn't even check your story, Yvonne, your bank withdrawals or anything. I wanted to walk into this today as a big enterprising sucker. I wanted you to keep this simple. Oh, you're just a piker in the setup, Abe. But I can imagine Yvonne is a pretty important member of the crew."

Yvonne bit her lip, trying to figure what he knew and how much.

"You know exactly who I'm talking about, don't you, honey? The blackmail crew that's gotten organized in this town. You're a member and J. X. O'Connell is a member. Who else?"

"You're insane," Yvonne said. "I'm an Odler—you can check that. Why should I—"

"Because you're also a slut and you get your kicks out of the business. Like those girlish pictures you gave me yesterday to warm my heart. Or were those to get money out of your own folks? Anyhow, you're a high-society hooker, honey. A priceless asset for your bunch because you circulate where there's pay dirt. And where there isn't any, you create it with your sweet face and your hot body and your stinking little soul." Thursday slopped her glass full again and snapped, "Drink! I'm getting ready to throw up just looking at you."

Her eyes watched him steadily over the glass rim. He said between his teeth, "I guess I'm losing my temper. I don't like you people making money off other people's mistakes. And I don't like you digging pits so mistakes can be made. Now you've learned something. You've learned a dumb private cop named Thursday is starting to nose around and he might be dangerous. Dangerous because he's unpredictable and because he's lucky in such matters." Even with the anger he was working up, he had to laugh inwardly at his boasting. But he knew the word about him was getting around and if he could make the word a little frightening, so much the better.

"You conceited ass," Yvonne said. Her voice was getting mushy. "You don't know what you're getting into."

"Don't kid yourself. I know and that's why I'm coming. Monday night your people tried to warn me off with Papago's hat. But I don't scare that easy. So they figured to give me Treatment B—the frame—and tie me up that way. That hasn't worked so well, either."

Abe keeled over on the divan. Yvonne's head was lolling on her chest. Thursday reached across the coffee table and held her chin up. He looked into her flickering eyes and spoke softly, on the chance that the loaded chartreuse had lowered her guard. "Somewhere in this town is the stuff that your people sell back to the owners. There's part of that material I want. Where's it kept?"

Yvonne tried to focus.

Thursday said, "Your people keep it locked up somewhere. Where? In a bank box or somebody's house? Who has the key?"

The girl's eyes wobbled and then got him in range. She drooled as she tried to spit at him.

Thursday stood up. "Okay. When you come out of this, tell your boss something for me. Tell your boss I'm coming after a handful of paper and if I have to tear up your business to get it, that won't break my heart. Got that?"

Yvonne got her drowsy head erect. "I got it," she slurred. "You wait."

She slid forward onto the floor, a sprawl of copper material and white legs. Thursday examined her eyes and then Abe's to make certain. Then he swiftly searched the apartment, removing his fingerprints as he went.

The place was clean, no address books, no diaries. All he found applicable were some more pictures of Yvonne and a notation in what was probably her handwriting on the telephone pad. The notation was two words: *Call Irene.*

Back in the living room, Thursday frowned over the prostrate forms of Abe and the girl. Then a cruel smile twitched at his mouth. He got to work again.

He took the chartreuse bottle out to the kitchen and poured the remainder down the drain. He rinsed out the bottle along with the glasses. After he had succeeded in planting the pair's fingerprints all over the glassware, he tossed it on the floor. Then he got Abe's straw hat and plaid coat and Speed Graphic from the bedroom.

After stripping Abe of everything but his striped shorts, he stretched the flabby body out on the divan. Then he flopped Yvonne next to the photographer and twined their unresisting arms around each other. When the sleepers were arranged to his liking, Thursday adjusted the camera and took two careful pictures.

He made a bundle of the hat and camera inside the coat and he was ready to go. His final act was to phone police headquarters. Adopting a southern accent, he identified himself to the desk sergeant as O. B. Hughes, one of the names he had read on the mailboxes below. He complained at length of the immoral goings-on in Apartment 2A and received assurance that an investigation would be made.

Carrying his bundle, he paused in the doorway to inspect his handiwork on the divan. For the first time since he had taken the client called Irene Whitney, he felt fairly pleased with himself. "*Thursday's Revenge,*" he said aloud. "Or, *The Biter Bit.*" He went out, leaving the door ajar for the police.

CHAPTER 13

WEDNESDAY, AUGUST 10, 3:30 P.M.

Thursday parked by the Army and Navy YMCA on the fringe of the nightclub district and changed into Abe's bright plaid coat. With the straw hat slanted over his eyes and the camera case under his arm, he slid out of his car and walked up Columbia.

The Don Kerner Photo Studio had been converted from a small garage into a quick-developer center for a string of photo girls. Thursday used the door in a plywood wall across what had been a driveway.

Inside, by a dusty gas pump, sat a war-surplus desk and a powdery aging blonde who was worried over a crossword puzzle. Two other younger women were reading movie magazines on a black-leather lounge against the brick wall. Nightclub camera girls, killing time before going on duty.

The blonde didn't look up past the Speed Graphic. She stopped sucking her pencil to say, "Boss man's in the darkroom. He's waiting for you."

Thursday grunted and kept going across the concrete floor toward another plywood partition that divided the gloomy building. He veered away from the nearest door, which was open. It led to a dressing room with make-up tables and a row of steel lockers.

A backward glance told him nobody was paying him any attention. He decided his best bet was the heavy curtain in the second doorway. He pushed the curtain aside and rapped on the inset door.

A man's muffled voice said, "Yeah?"

"Abe," Thursday answered, trying to approximate the photographer's voice.

"Just a second," the man said. Thursday remembered to pull the curtain to behind him and waited, listening to movement within the darkroom. "Okay—come on in."

Thursday stepped into the absolute blackness and groped the door shut behind him. The other man switched on the red bulb over the sink. The dim shape of an enlarger seemed to leap at Thursday's head.

"Been sweating you out," Don Kerner said, wiping his hands on a paper towel. "She's phoned a couple times in the last half hour."

Thursday grunted as the safest form of communication and stayed by the door beyond the faint illumination. He had seen Kerner somewhere before. He was a big untidy man with a paunch and light hair and a heavy upper lip.

"Come on—give." He took the camera impatiently and pulled out the plate holder. "Hope you got something good." He turned out the light again.

Thursday stood still in the pitch dark while Kerner worked, praying the other man would drop a hint he could use. *She's* phoned, Kerner had said. That was a beginning.

Kerner's high-pitched voice came out of the blackness. "May be another job for you right away. Tonight."

Thursday grunted, "Oh?" as a leader.

"Yeah. Some little snob. Going to use the beach party setup."

Thursday smiled for his own benefit, doubting whether that routine would ever come off after today's work.

Then Kerner said, "You stick around, Abe, till I get these printed and you can run them over to night and day for me yourself. She's got ants in her pants."

"Uh-huh," Thursday murmured. *She*, again. And *night and day*. He felt a glow of fierce joy. Here were facts he could close his hands around.

"Beats me what the grand rush is," Kerner complained. "Everybody's in too big a hurry these days, it seems to me." He turned on the red light again and with wooden tongs lifted the dripping negatives out of the developer and plunged them into the hypo tray. "Now we'll see what cooks."

Silently, Thursday inched away from the door, moving behind the photographer. Kerner bent over the hypo, studying the negatives and humming to himself. His humming stopped short and he bent even closer to the pan, not believing his eyes.

There was a moment in the darkroom when no one breathed. Then Kerner's bulk came to life. Grabbing up the tray of developer acid with both hands, he whirled and flung it at the door—where Thursday had been standing.

He never realized his mistake. Thursday smashed him in the mouth and cracked him a second time on the side of the jaw. As Kerner fell back against the big suspended enlarger, Thursday went with him, his fingers after the man's windpipe. They hit the floor together, along with the enlarger, and Thursday got up off the unconscious body.

He listened by the door for two minutes. Kerner had made no sound but some equipment had crashed around. Nobody came, and Thursday wondered what one had to do to raise a crowd in this place.

He used the electric cord from the broken enlarger to bind Kerner's hands and feet, and some paper toweling as a gag. Finally, he was satisfied that the photographer couldn't interfere with his plans for a little while, barring accidents.

Brown manila envelopes were piled on one of the shelves. Thursday took one and folded two others inside as filler. Before he switched off the light, he glanced at the pictures of Yvonne and Abe and was gratified to find that they were good sharp negatives.

On the way out, Thursday hesitated by the desk, holding the brown envelope so it partially masked his face. "Don says he doesn't want to be disturbed for anything."

The blonde shrugged over the word she was erasing from her puzzle. "Don't worry, guy. I keep the body out of darkrooms."

The two picture snatchers tittered appreciatively and Thursday went out. He filed Abe's hat and coat and the envelopes in the trash can beside his car.

Chapter 14

WEDNESDAY, AUGUST 10, 4:00 P.M.

The line in the YMCA's phone book read *Night & Day agcy Bnk Amer Bldg*. Thursday began to undergo the cold excitement of success. He dodged his sedan up Broadway to Sixth where the Bank of America Building towered over downtown. It was just a block from his own office.

He was the only passenger for the sixth floor where an elderly man was tapping his cane, impatient for the elevator. As the elderly man got on, he nodded to Thursday getting off. Thursday nodded back absently and looked over the various office doors.

Then he whirled around. The elderly man had known his face, hadn't placed it immediately and so had made the mistake of nodding as to an acquaintance. But it wasn't as an acquaintance he knew Thursday.

Through the closing doors of the elevator Thursday saw the dignified face of J. X. O'Connell, horror-struck at his error. Then the crack narrowed to nothing over the glimpse, and the dial above the elevator doors spun swiftly from 6 to 1.

Thursday couldn't even find it in himself to swear. He had gotten the biggest break in the world but it had been timed a little too fast for him. Almost before he fully realized what he had missed, his quarry was lost in the quitting-time crowd on Broadway.

So he smiled wryly and went looking for the right door, the door that O'Connell had undoubtedly just used. It turned out to be a double door and something special for the staid building. It was black with silver fittings, too deliberately impressive.

Thursday pushed through into a large waiting room that was also painted black and carpeted in a silver gray that exactly matched the nap of the low-slung furniture. No one was waiting. Thursday sauntered past two glass-walled interviewing booths to where the receptionist sat with typewriter and PBX board behind a glass barrier.

She was a pretty girl wearing an orchid whose edges were beginning to curl. She smiled nicely and asked to help him.

"I'm looking for a butler," Thursday explained. Behind her, in the office section, he could see a half dozen more girls, all good-looking, busy at desk work.

"I see," the receptionist said. "I'm afraid that—we're not really an employment agency, you know, except in exceptional cases where our clients—"

"I understand that. But this is an exceptional case and your woman thought she could help me out."

"Oh, in that case." She plugged a connection on the PBX board. "Won't you please sit down for a moment while I see if she's busy? May I have your name, sir?"

"Max Thursday." He sank into the nearest bouncy chair. On either side of the room, by the glass barrier, was a single black door. The silver letters on one read MR. RUPERT, the other MISS DAY. Thursday was banking on Miss Day being Kerner's *she*.

He plucked an illustrated brochure from the neat rack of magazines. "What Is Night & Day?" Thursday opened to read the explanatory message. He smiled when the brochure told him that the firm sold personal services. "Let us act for you when the need arises. . . ." The services included such varied jobs as meeting trains, buying Christmas gifts, serving legal papers, compiling statistics, catering for parties, and standing in at proxy marriages. ". . . since 1944."

The receptionist said Miss Day would see him now.

He went into Miss Day's office, more silvery tones against black, and the woman rose from behind her black desk to come around and shake hands. "I'm Quincy Day," she said in a voice like a lullaby. "So pleasant of you to come to see me, Mr. Thursday. Please sit down. I'm sorry you had to wait but—" her soft strong hand slipped out of his to riffle across the cluttered desk top "—this paper work! Business would be so simple if one didn't find it necessary to record one's brain on invoices and so many, many memoranda."

She made him comfortable. Physically, anyway. Instinctively, he had already started to fight with himself. He knew what she was and how he intended to have her end up, by his own hand if possible. But, shouting against all the facts, the impulsiveness which was his worst enemy told him to like her. She radiated a warm human enchantment that got him.

He watched her make the return trip around her desk on extremely high heels—for a tall woman—which flattered the full contours of her legs. He said dryly, "But the key word of business is distrust. So you must write things down."

She said, "I'm afraid so," and took the pencil out of her black upswept hair, and the harlequin glasses away from her round face. It wasn''t the rakish frames of the glasses that had made Thursday see her as a streamlined, friendly witch. Quincy Day had heavy slanting eyebrows and violet slanting eyes, and there were no lobes to her tiny ears. She was sleeky plump. Her smooth bare ivory neck flowed into a black crepe frock that was adorned only by her being inside it and by an ornate gold Q on her left shoulder.

"However, there are benefits," she said. "If you discovered a way to make people trust one another and eliminated the keeping of records, think how many of us would be bereft of employment." Her smile was broad, cheerful, and candid.

"Oh, people generally find a way to create a job where there isn't one." Thursday tried the same kind of smile. "Like Night & Day, for instance. San Diego struggled along for three hundred years without you. But now . . ."

"How true!" She poised her pencil. "Now let us hope we may prove indispensable to you too, Mr. Thursday."

"You are already."

"Splendid. Since the need already exists, then we don't have to scour our minds trying to create one. Instead, we face the comparatively simple task of finding the solution."

"Night & Day," said Thursday. "Who plays Night in the combination?"

She waggled her pencil impatiently but smiled. "Oh, more

than once I've regretted choosing that particular name, although it fulfills the requirements: short, easy to remember and epitomizing service. No, there is no Night, Mr. Thursday, merely an attempt at cleverness. Now, what may we do for you?"

"I'm looking for a butler."

"So Marie told me. But as she told you, or should have told you—"

"Night & Day is not really an employment agency, except in exceptional cases where our clients something-or-other," he quoted.

"To the letter. Therefore—"

"But I have a rather special spot for a rather special butler. In fact, there's no place else I could go and be sure of getting satisfaction."

"Do go on, Mr. Thursday."

He linked his fingers behind his head and said dreamily, "I see a picture of what I want in my mind. A tall man with a poker up his back. Gray hair, and a gray mustache that looks like a fine old toothbrush. A guy who might pass for a gentleman anywhere, except that a real live gentleman would think he was a little overdressed with his white gloves and bamboo cane."

In the silence, Quincy's eyes darkened to purple. She murmured, "You're quite particular."

"I can afford to be. I know that such a guy exists and from his looks he has to be a butler or has been a butler. I've got great confidence in Night & Day. I'm sure you can put your finger on him if anybody can."

The phone buzzed. Quincy said, "Excuse me," and answered it. She listened to the other party impassively, her eyes still locked with Thursday's, pencil tapping softly. Finally she said, "I already know. No, I don't know how. Thank you for calling."

She hung up and began, "Mr. Thursday, I'm extremely sorry not to justify your confidence in Night & Day but I do fear—" The phone buzzed again. Again she put the receiver to her ear and listened serenely. But with this call she leaned back in her chair and took a deep breath and the pencil picked up tempo. "You're too late," she said into the mouthpiece, "much too late," and hung up again.

"An indispensable instrument, the telephone," Thursday said and let her study him.

Quincy stood up abruptly and slipped the pencil back into her hairdo. "I'm sorry not to be able to help you. If you'll leave your name with our receptionist and where you can be reached, I'll call you if something should arise. Meanwhile, several matters really need my personal attention—" she was circling the desk "—and so if you'll excuse me . . ."

Thursday stayed in the chair and said, "The first call was from O'Connell and the second from Kerner. Or vice versa."

Quincy stopped dead and flipped a switch on the intercom. She told it, "Rupert—I need you." Her tongue between her teeth, she gave Thursday a lazy smile.

The office door opened and a short man padded in. He was a fat forty, innocuous and rabbit-faced. Wearing a bursting vest but no coat, he appeared to be the firm's accountant.

The woman commanded, "Rupert, throw this man out."

Rupert's mild eyes flickered and his pursy mouth drooped sadly. He looked at Thursday's long wiry body and he inquired, "What do you mean, Quincy dear?"

"Precisely what I said. This man is annoying me. Get rid of him."

"I see." Rupert paled and his cheek twitched. "Certainly. I advise you to run along, sir, and not make a scene. You heard what—"

Thursday got up easily and ambled slowly toward the little barrel of man. Rupert bit his lip and shifted his feet indecisively. "Now just a minute," he argued nervously. "There's no cause in our acting uncivilized about this."

"Rupert!"

Thursday closed his hand gently on Rupert's necktie and backed him out through the doorway. He said, "You'll have to pardon me," and shut the door in Rupert's face and shot the bolt. Then he turned to Quincy Day and said, "Please don't embarrass me like that again."

Her mouth, sensual a few minutes before, was now a narrow exasperated line. "I'll call the police. There's no reason I—"

"The number is Franklin 1101."

"You don't believe I will? Then you're daring me to—"?

"You know your business better than I do." And Thursday sat down again.

Furiously, she snatched up the receiver and ordered the receptionist to get her the number. Thursday listened attentively to her wordy complaint of being molested by a strange man in her office and lit a cigarette.

She slammed the phone together and clasped her hands and asked, "Does that prove anything to you, Mr. Thursday?"

"No. Except that you chatter too much. Cigarette?"

"Indeed? Let me say that—" She clamped her mouth together again in that ugly line he didn't like and flounced behind her desk to sit down.

Thursday puffed out a little smoke screen between them. "Let me chatter a minute—about gypsies, since you might be one. You know, the only real monarchy left in the world belongs to the Kalo Roms."

Quincy stared stonily at the locked door behind him. Thursday picked a fleck of tobacco off his lower lip. "This case that comes to mind, the queen regent had died up near San Berdoo. She didn't leave any kids, an unusual situation among gypsies which I won't bother to explain to you, Quincy. Consequently, a lot of families started wrangling about who'd take over."

Below on Broadway the sound of a siren died away to a moan. Thursday said, "The Budvano clan won the title but the Maravlasis—another big outfit—called cops, claiming the queen had been murdered for her job. A detective friend of mine was hired by said Budvanos to dig into the mess and turn up facts favorable to their cause, and, as it finally came out, they were innocent, all right. But the Maravlasis weren't;

they were running heroin on the side. So they don't do much gypsying any more. I guess it doesn't pay to call cops if you got anything to hide."

An open hand banged at the door. Thursday put out his cigarette and got up to unbolt it.

Rupert peered over the policeman's shoulder.

Thursday laughed and sat down again. "Are you assigned to me special, Hoover?"

Rupert stayed in the doorway. Hoover stalked in, eyeing Thursday suspiciously, but taking his hand off his persuader. "There's supposed to be a Miss Day here. I got a call on the radio—"

Quincy swept around to him, beaming. "I'm Quincy Day, officer. While I'm thoroughly impressed by your alacrity, I'm very much afraid you've had all your trouble for nothing, although I do appreciate your promptness ever so much."

"Yeah?" Hoover looked Thursday over doubtfully. "I still have to know what's been going on."

"A slight misunderstanding," Quincy soothed. "But all taken care of now. Mr. Rupert here, my associate, apparently had a few too many and tried to pick a fight with Mr. Thursday. I became frightened and I—well—" she was helplessly feminine and Thursday wanted to applaud "—I suppose I called for the police when I shouldn't."

Hoover grunted. "This on the level, Thursday?"

"You heard the lady."

Rupert's mouth hung open. Quincy regarded him sorrowfully. "I'm certain Rupert is ready to apologize for his part in this, and Mr. Thursday has very graciously decided not to press charges. So you see, officer—it was really foolish of me to bother you. I do hope you'll forgive me."

Hoover scanned them all once again. Then he shrugged, tight-lipped. He made a brief entry in his report book and said to Thursday, "I go off duty at six. Can you get through the night without me?" And as he passed by Rupert: "Next time you pick a fight stay in your own class, fellow."

Quincy followed him into the waiting room, apologizing profusely. When she came back, she jerked her sleek head at Rupert. "Get out."

"I only did—"

"I know." Quincy pushed him out of the way and closed the door and came over to lean against the desk front by Thursday. Her slant eyes darkened again as she glowered down at him over her bosom. She looked now as a witch should look. Her words came out in a low hiss. "What is it you want?"

He had never seen so much hate in a face so tranquil. He smiled up at her ruefully. "Funny, I like you personally. I don't know how this may come out, whether I salt you down in prison or the gas chamber. It won't make any difference to that, but I like you."

"No, it won't make one bit of difference. However, that's not what I asked. *What is it you want?*"

Thursday got up gravely. He put a little-kid kiss on the tip of his forefinger and planted it lightly on her nose. Quincy didn't flinch and her baleful eyes didn't let go of his. He murmured, "A butler," and left her.

CHAPTER 15

WEDNESDAY, AUGUST 10, 5:00 P.M.

Thursday put in a brief appearance at his own office to see what sort of a message Irene Whitney had left. She hadn't left any; there was no indication that she had tried to get in touch with him. He couldn't figure that out. Monday he had watched the anxiety bubble under her veneer of self-control. Yet two days had passed since she had shown any interest in her ten IOUs.

He suddenly dialed a number and said, "This is Max. Stick around. I'm coming over." He wangled his car through the homing press of traffic to the Spreckels Building.

John D. Meier was a short powerful man in his mid-thirties with black bushy eyebrows and a fierce doubting smile. He was perched on the edge of his secretary's desk drumming his heels when Thursday walked in.

"Can you read?" was his abrupt greeting.

Thursday grinned and flopped on the waiting bench. "Sure. The sign says Insurance Claims Investigations. You afraid of work?"

"The sign also says office hours 9 to 5. Saturdays 9 to 1. What kind of favor you after this time, Thursday?"

"You're uncanny, John. Look, you've got access to some information I might need. I mean the national insurance cross files. It'll be a big help if you pull a check for me. I'm onto a female who seems hipped on the photography angle of easy money and I think you might have something on her, if you'll be so wonderfully kind as to look."

"Well, don't break down and cry. What's her name?"

"I'll bet it isn't hers so let's not fog the issue. She's five-eight, under thirty by not very much, with kind of oriental eyes, violet-colored. That's the unchangeable stuff. She's also a brunette, hundred and forty pounds, but stacked just dandy."

Meier chuckled. "Never mind her name. What's her phone number?"

"You don't like gabby women. How about the check?"

"I can try. But photography. For a *modus operandi* that sounds more like shakedown than insurance fraud."

"What makes you say so?"

"I've got it on the brain. Say, how about the cops? Can't you work through your buddy Clapp?"

"Not at this point, John. You see, we're good enough friends to protect each other. He wouldn't slip me anything that might involve his integrity and I don't make him keep any of my secrets."

"How sweet." Meier jumped down off the desk, made a note on a scratch pad and stuffed it in his pocket. "Uninvolved as I may be, I got to admit you couldn't have caught me at a worse time. Come on, let's get this show on the road."

They rode down in the elevator together. "Busy?" Thursday asked.

"This Showalter smashup has got me talking to myself."

"Perry Showalter? I read about it."

"What do you know! It's only been page one since a week ago when he skidded his car off Torrey Pines grade. He was loaded with insurance. Only natural for a guy in his position."

They got off the elevator. "He skidded the car, huh? Not the car skidded. You know what that sounds like?"

"It sounds like what I'm talking about, Thursday. Suicide. The papers don't know. But I've established he was despondent and I'm going to establish the rest of it—the reason."

"You going to break his policies on the suicide clause?"

"No. They're beyond the limitations." Meier quoted singsong, "If the insured, whether sane or insane, shall die by his or her own hand or act within one year from the date hereof, this policy shall be void and shall have no value—but in such event the company will return the premium paid, end of sentence." He chuckled. "No, I'm out to break the double indemnity, that's all. Suicide is no accident."

"Don't you ever get tired of robbing widows, John?"

"I do. But suicide is still no accident. Us ghouls have regulations. And Showalter was despondent for a good and sufficient reason, according to Benedict and me."

"Benedict? Is he in it?"

"Figure this one out. Showalter owned one of the biggest, most profitable hardware stores in San Diego. Social leader. Prominent yachtsman. Worth piles." Meier punched Thursday's stomach. "But he's got practically no money left that we can find."

"Well, well," Thursday murmured. "That's why you've got blackmail on the brain."

"Yup. Family's lucky he accumulated all that insurance. Otherwise, they'd be next to broke since the store turned out to be in hock. That's what we figure Showalter figured—kill himself before he had to cash in the insurance policies too." Meier shrugged and grinned. "I should feel sorry for a guy like that. Well, take care of yourself, Thursday. Call me or I'll call you."

"Right." Thursday watched Meier's stocky figure march off to his automobile. After a moment, he turned and went slowly to find his own. He drove home to his duplex, showered, shaved, and picked up Merle Osborn at her apartment a little before seven. Off duty, she affected less masculinity. She softened her voice and wore a dress that draped beguilingly and let her hair down in a dusty-brown cloud around her face. "The Disguise" was their standing joke.

They ate dinner in a candlelit booth at the Cotton Patch. When they had rinsed their fingers clean of the barbecued spareribs, Merle challenged him with her round eyes.

"Talk up, kiddo."

"About what?"

"About anything of current interest. You're getting to be just like a doctor. You're so used to playing the smug act for everybody—simply crawling with inside information—that you can't relax. I'm no client, you know."

He chuckled. "What I got to be smug about, I don't know. But I must be, since Clapp said so yesterday and you said so right now."

"Oh, forget it." She took his hand across the table. "I'm just picky. I feel left out."

"Left out of what?"

"Out of some trouble you're in. I know that bemused look of yours."

"I'm bemused, all right. Got any J. X. O'Connell?"

"Not a word. My files don't know the name."

"Got any Quincy Day?"

Merle didn't say anything right away. Then she forced a laugh. "Pardon my girlish jealousy. I did a feature on her when she opened—an extra assignment, nothing in the crime line." She paused, gazing dolefully at him between the candles. "Say, you've got a nice-looking client there, haven't you?"

"Don't let it worry you, honey."

"Me? I don't worry about women. I worry about the gay way you do business. I worry about small artillery."

"I don't carry any; I won't meet any. That's my axiom since—you know when." He squeezed her fingers. "Actually. I'm not shutting you out of a thing. I got nothing but hunches on a job that doubles its size every time I turn around. Don't breathe it to a soul, but the great Thursday doesn't know where he is at."

"Okay, okay." She grinned and made a kiss at him. "But keep that thick head covered, huh, boy? The D.A. is waiting behind the door with an axe."

"Osborn—if I worried about all the people who hated my guts I'd never have won the war. If you think Benedict's a fan, you should have seen my C.O. Why, the day I took Saipan . . ."

She let him ramble through the entire story before she said, "Yes, you told me."

Later, when they walked through the balmy night to his Oldsmobile, he said, "Here's a hunch."

She bumped closer to him. "What I think it is?"

"No. This involves a war of attrition and a tip for you. Don't let on that it's a tip. But suppose you nose deeper into the Showalter story, the financial side. I'd like to see that get some publicity."

"Okay, but I don't feel very newsy right now," Merle added tentatively. "I claim there's beer in a certain loose lady's refrigerator, plus soda for the loose lady's scotch. Want to check that lead, copper?"

He patted her. "Not tonight, Osborn, I'm going to make me a big day tomorrow and that calls for some eight hours of sacktime."

"Okay, I guess I'll have to destroy the evidence myself. If you find you can't sleep . . ."

"Not tonight. Don't be lonesome."

"Me?" She fluffed up her back hair elaborately. "What's one dumb detective more or less? Where I come from, we use them for bait."

CHAPTER 16

THURSDAY, AUGUST 11, 9:00 A.M.

The Sentinel on his doorstep the next morning had nothing to say about Yvonne Odler or the photographer Abe. Nor did the *Union* which Thursday bought in the lobby of the Moulton Building. He wasn't surprised, knowing the power of the Odler name.

Fred, counting his change across the cigarstand counter, had the only news. He muttered, "Lady went up about eight-thirty."

"What kind of lady?"

"The blonde—the high-hat one you said keep an eye out for."

Thursday went up and opened his office. He sat behind his desk and pretended to be amazed when Irene Whitney came in at three minutes after nine. She took the client chair without a word, nodding her hello and waiting coolly for him to speak.

He said, "Nice day, isn't it, Miss Whitney?"

She puckered her mouth quizzically and considered and

said in her clipped way, "Yes, I believe it will be." She wore a linen suit of canary yellow with gloves, belt, and shoes of white. She was not at all nervous.

"It was a nice day Tuesday. Might I ask you why you couldn't give me a ring?"

"I stopped by here about half-past three Tuesday afternoon. Your office was locked and I thought better of leaving a message."

"I figured all that hocus-pocus Monday in Loma Portal was to avoid connecting yourself with this office. You change your mind?"

"Somewhat. Monday, I handled matters so poorly and put myself in such a ridiculous light that—well . . ."

"At least, we're coming along. Now why the lack of interest yesterday?"

"Really, Mr. Thursday!" Her slow-spreading smile softened her aristocratic face. "Wasn't Wednesday a dangerous day for anyone to show interest in you? Please, may I have them now?"

Thursday frowned. "Have what?"

Her smile stiffened, a bit haughtily. "Don't play, please. I *am* taking a risk coming here at all—more of a risk than you'll ever know. Please give me my IOUs."

"I don't have them." The assurance on her face didn't fade during the moment of stillness, so Thursday thought she hadn't heard and said it again.

"But in the papers—the murder! Papago was killed, wasn't he? Naturally, I assumed—"

"—that I murdered him to recover your IOUs and earn your lousy fee." Thursday laughed, a quick bitter sound. "Naturally, you'd assume that. Tell me, will you find it necessary to bathe immediately upon leaving this office?"

She said, as a matter of form, "I apologize. I didn't mean quite that."

"Not quite. You didn't mean for me to get insulted at the idea of taking your money for killing a man. I apologize if I seem touchy, Miss Whitney. But you've got the same crumby ideas about my character as Papago's mistress and she's a little beneath your class. Let's get it straight: I didn't kill George Papago for your gambling debts or any other reason."

"Then who—" she began faintly.

Thursday said, "Shortly before you hired me, a man using the name of J. X. O'Connell called on Papago. He represented himself as your lawyer, paid for the IOUs and made off with them. When I saw Papago, all I succeeded in doing was to needle his ingrown cupidity. He smelled easy money so he went out to find O'Connell himself. He found him and O'Connell beat his head in. That's a progress report, Miss Whitney."

Now the fright blurred her clean-cut features. The padded shoulders of her yellow suit went up and down rapidly with her breathing. "How—that's ghastly!"

"Yes, it's ghastly, and it's also confidential. Not that you want to have anything to do with the police."

"No, of course not—never! But this means she really does have my IOUs."

"Then you've heard from your woman again."

"Last evening. She telephoned during dinner and told me I had only until next week. I wasn't too much upset because I was certain that you already—" she bit at the seam of a glove finger, lost "—had them," she remembered to finish.

"Next week. To scrape your payment together?"

"In a way," Irene said guardedly.

Thursday shook his head exasperatedly. "Who are you the most afraid of—her or me? You don't seem very accustomed to lying, at least you do a punk job of it, so why don't you give me a decent chance to help you? What's this hold she has over you?"

Her light-blue eyes pleaded with dignity. "I daren't tell you that," she whispered. "Mr. Thursday, ask me anything else."

"Okay. Is this mystery woman Yvonne Odler?"

Her mouth fell slightly apart. "Good heavens, no! What do you know about Yvonne Odler?"

"What do you know about her?"

"I didn't say that I knew anything about her. You introduced her name into the conversation."

Thursday banged his palms wearily on the edge of the desk and got up. He went over to the window and stood rubbing the back of his neck while he squinted at the hot clean morning sky. "Look, Miss Whitney. Your little recovery case has turned into a murder case which I don't belong in. I'm getting under the D.A.'s feet where I also don't belong because I'm liable to lose my temper at that righteous pillar, which act would benefit him only. I'm up against a small army of shakedown artists. Isn't that enough trouble without my being up against my client, too?" She didn't answer and he didn't look around at her. He said, droning, "Either you level with me or we'll call it quits."

"You mean you'd withdraw and leave me helpless?"

"I'm doing just that."

"No." He heard her chair rasp the floor as she rose. Her voice came closer, the chopped tones having difficulty conveying the emotion she wanted to convey. "Mr. Thursday—Max—I'm not accustomed to begging, either, but I'm begging with you now. Please don't—please—"

He turned around and she was standing in front of him, kneading her purse. He looked down at the perfect part in her blonde hair. She wore her hair skinned back functionally, like Merle Osborn but neater. He asked, "Why not?"

"Because I *am* helpless. I'm so alone in this and I need you desperately."

"Not enough to trust me with facts. For example: Tuesday afternoon you drove by the alligator farm where Papago's body was found. Nobody knew about Papago at the time except me and the cops. But you slowed down and stared and stared. How did *you* know?"

Irene raised her eyes. They were steady, if the smile she was trying to wear on her pink mouth flickered. She moistened her lips and murmured. "Max, can't you just trust me? Not my actions, just *me*?"

"If I trusted like that, I'd be deader than Papago, and he's three days dead. You've got to do more than cross your heart."

"What can I say?"

"The truth."

Her frightened face was lifted. She stepped her small straight body nearer so that it touched his at hips and chest. The passionate curl to her mouth was a horrible joke and so was her voice, crooning. "Max—don't I mean anything to you? Won't you—mayn't I offer you anything to help me?"

"I have your retainer."

"But I mean—" the cords of her throat tautened, choking her "—I didn't mean—" she burst away from him and turned her back, and the padded yellow shoulders shuddered with her sobbing. "I can't do it!" she moaned. "I can't do it!"

Thursday said softly, "Of course, you can't. There's a hundred things you aren't accustomed to and abridgement of self-respect seems to top the list. You're clumsier at that than at lying. I'm glad to have it proved because I thought from the beginning that you were quite a nice lady. Now blow your nose and stop calling yourself names and—"

The telephone shrilled. He swung it up. "Thursday speaking."

Silence. Then the other party began babbling and Thursday thought it was a woman. Only when the scared cataract of words began to make some sense did he realize it was Don Kerner's high-pitched voice. The photographer ran out of breath with. "Thursday, I've got to see you!"

"Calm down. You've got my address."

"I can't come there. It's out of the question. I can't go anywhere. I've got to see you. Thursday, right away!"

"Why?"

Kerner's panting labored through the receiver. He began saying over and over, "They're after me! They're going to kill me!"

"Shut up!" Thursday snapped. "Where you phoning from? Is your car there?"

"Rexall place, Twelfth and Market. My car's not here. It's still—"

"Anyone tailing you?"

"No, I don't think so. But I know what they're—"

"Okay, listen. Grab a bus and get down to the Coronado ferry. Ride back and forth on the top deck until I get there. Understand?"

"Yeah," Kerner said. "Yeah, I can do that. But be—"

Thursday broke the connection and looked at Irene Whitney. She had repaired her face and she lingered by the client chair as if it gave her strength. But her chin was up with its former hauteur. "I won't annoy you by apologizing at length but I am completely sorry. You've been perfectly fine and I've behaved very badly. I understand about your position, your business, and I'll send you payment in full. Please don't worry any more about my affairs, I don't intend that. Perhaps my problem isn't as difficult as I've—"

"Call me tomorrow," he said. "I wasn't teasing out your speech just to hear it all—I've been reconsidering. But please call."

She said firmly. "Are you certain it's right to continue? I mean, what I'm trying not to do is jeopardize your business sense out of regard for my being a woman."

"What business sense?" He grinned. "Granted I like you, Miss Whitney, even when you wipe your feet on me. But that's the least of my whims."

"Then what—"

He plucked his hat off the consumer. "There's nasty people picking on you and they've insulted me. I guess I'm spoiling for a fight."

Chapter 17

THURSDAY, AUGUST 11, 10:00 A.M.

He circled the top deck of the ferry twice after the boarding whistle had hooted. The taste of the harbor breeze was good in Thursday's throat but there was no Don Kerner. He made a strolling perusal of the automobile deck with no better results. So he returned up top and simply had a ride, leaning on the rail and watching the sea gulls attack the glaring water for garbage. He had left his Oldsmobile in the police headquarters parking lot which was a block from the San Diego ferry slip.

The bulky craft disgorged at Coronado, reloaded, hooted some more and made the return trip. Thursday sat on a bench and watched another batch of city passengers file aboard. He looked for the paunchy, blond, smooth-shaven man he remembered from a picture long ago.

He nearly missed his man. Don Kerner was a redhead; he wore a ragged red mustache. Thursday chuckled and privately blessed darkroom lights everywhere. It had been the red developer bulb yesterday that had let him see through Kerner's altered face. The rosy light had made his hair as colorless as in the old days; the light had faded the new mustache back into the upper lip. "Luck," he reminded himself gently. "Luck, not brains."

Kerner's baggy figure marched on by him and collapsed on a bench a few yards away. Thursday inspected the people who boarded behind the photographer but they seemed harmless enough. When the ramp gate closed he moved over beside Kerner and said, "Start talking. Keep it soft."

Kerner's hands wouldn't stay still. When they weren't scratching the red mustache, they were wiping themselves on his creaseless trousers. He hadn't shaved yet today and he looked like a D.T. vag case. It was coward's fright. He talked.

"Who's they?" Thursday cut in when the jerky sentences began to repeat.

"Night & Day. You know—you were there. That's the reason. They think it's my fault you got that far. That I should have stopped you. How? How could I when—"

"They tell you this?"

"No, no," moaned Kerner. "They didn't tell me anything. Not a thing."

"What makes you so worried, then?"

"I called them on the phone a dozen times. Yesterday. This morning. They won't talk to me. I went there myself an hour ago. Nobody'd see me. The girl kept lying, kept saying they were out. She didn't know when they'd be in. But it was a lie. I could hear that Quincy's voice through the door. She was being sweet to some customer while everybody lied to me, Thursday." Kerner tried to hold his hands together in his lap. "She's poison. I'm marked, Thursday. I know it. They're going to get rid of me. You know there's only one safe way to get rid of me. They'll do it!"

"Maybe and maybe not. Where do I fit in?"

"You got to help me. See, you help me and I'll help you. I don't want to start running. I'm getting old." Kerner grabbed his arm and then released it swiftly, not wanting to hazard any chances of presumption. "You got to help me because I only know one trade. They'd track me through that. I got no place to go."

"No, they'd find you, all right," Thursday said. "I *can* help. The question is—do I want to?"

"You got to want to! What am I supposed to do? Wait around Dago here and take it?"

"What do you know that I'd like to know?"

"Anything—anything. Just ask me anything." Kerner begged.

"Keep your voice down. Start with you."

"Me?" Kerner stared vaguely out at an aircraft carrier in midchannel. "I'm nobody, just Don Kerner. I've had that photography setup on Columbia for a couple years now. Before that I did some movie work up north and got laid off. I never knew what she was letting me in for, until it was too late. You got to believe that, so help me!"

Thursday said flatly, "You're a liar, so help me. Before you became Don Kerner, you were Don Cornish, alias Don Cornwall, alias Sam Pierce, alias I don't know what all. You served out five years at San Quentin for extortion involving pictures when you double-crossed the tart who helped you work the tourist camps around Sacramento. Your movie experience consists of seeing one a week along with the rest of your cell block."

"No, that's wrong—"

"Wrong, thinking hair dye and a mustache and a bigger belly could cover up a cheap roper like you. Once you're mugged, you're mugged for good." Thursday stood up scornfully. "See, I found out whether you'd throw me a curve or not. I'm not going to fall in pulling you out."

The ferry was banging into the Coronado slip again. Kerner turned his sagging face up and clutched at Thursday's coat. "All right, all right," he implored brokenly. "It's a lie, I admit that. You know me. But the rest of it's true. You got to listen to me, Thursday."

"To another bedtime story?" But Thursday sat down again and had a cigarette, waiting for Kerner to come out of it. The other man had an attack of trembling and wiped his hand across his damp face.

"No more bedtime stories. Straight goods," Kerner said with an effort. "You must have a terrific memory. I got sprung in '40. Drifted around, going straight, finally set up here in Dago. For a while, everything fine. Then this Night & Day came around with a proposition—she knew about me, too. It was big money and there isn't much of that on the level, so I started handling their business."

"Extortion again."

"Sure, bigtime. My nightclub girls worked right in with it,

though they never knew. They'd get a picture of Joe Blow out with some other guy's wife. Night & Day would collect. And they work with a couple doctors and psychiatrists around town, people spilling out their troubles. They got a tie-in with a couple national lonely-hearts sucker lists. Bellboys, too, and some callgirls and back drivers and a bartender or two—all fingering for them." Kerner shivered and whispered for himself, "It's big."

"Who's the boss?"

Kerner looked surprised. "Her, Quincy Day, I told you."

Thursday laughed. "I'm just trying to figure what you might have for sale. I could have gotten this far with a ouija board, Kerner."

"I'm getting to it. I'm getting to it." Kerner took a deep breath and huddled closer to Thursday and mumbled. "Copies of everything Night & Day is doing business with. Can you use that stuff?"

Thursday began to smile off at space. "You improve with age."

"It works this way. First, Night & Day lets the sucker know they got something on him. Then they send him a photo copy to prove it. He pays so much every month to keep it under cover—regular invoices and everything. When I joined up, I saw it might be smart to pull my own copy of all the stuff. I got it all stashed away in a locker club downtown under another name."

"Kerner, you ought to be analyzed. You got perfect rat psychology."

"Is the stuff worth anything to you?"

"How'd you manage to stay alive this long? All this time you've been working for shakedown people and looking forward to shaking *them* down. Here's the time come and you're scared spitless."

"But is it worth anything to *you*?" Kerner whined, tugging at Thursday's arm.

Thursday jerked away from him. Then he sighed. He said,

"Lucky I got an end in view or I'd never come down to your level. You bring your stuff back here. I'll do what I can to save your life, though I think it's a waste of time."

When the ferry berthed on the San Diego side, Don Kerner slunk ashore and caught the bus headed uptown. Thursday roamed around the top deck, smoking and wondering if he would ever see Kerner again. But two crossings later the man was back, a bulging manila envelope under his coat.

The noon rush had started now and more passengers were flocking aboard. They found a secluded spot forward and Kerner fidgeted while Thursday examined the photo copies one by one. Occasionally the detective raised his eyebrows or whistled softly but otherwise he was deathly silent.

"Well?" Kerner demanded finally. "Is that good or isn't it?" There was a sniggering pride in his voice.

Thursday spit over the side and eyed him, and the photographer began to deflate. Thursday said, "Don't get cocky or I'll toss you to the sea gulls. Where are the originals for this crud?"

"I don't know. Maybe they're in her office—that's where I send them back to and that's where the invoice files are. Where Night & Day keeps the hot stuff, I don't know."

"Okay. You've done your part so I'll do mine. Come on. We'll get off in Coronado."

He ignored Kerner's attempts to whisper nervous questions as they debarked. With the other man at his heels, Thursday strode down the ramp into the terminal and the nearest telephone booth. He dialed the Coronado police station.

"My name is Max Thursday." The desk sergeant didn't know him so he recited his private license number. "I'm down at your ferry terminal. I want to prefer assault charges against a bum who just got rough. I'll hold him here for a prowl car."

Kerner tried to get away.

Thursday caught him by the magazine stand and dragged

him toward the shadow of a pillar, away from the curious passengers boarding. Kerner whimpered, "Let me go! You're trying to cross me—I heard you!" He twisted and threw a clumsy punch into Thursday's mouth.

Thursday snarled, "Shut up!" and bent Kerner's arm up behind. "I'll do this thing my way. Jail's the place you'll be safest. Let them book you under a phony name—James Donald—and keep your mouth shut. In a couple of days, or as soon as it's safe, I'll drop the charges and that'll be that. Don't try anything with the cops or they'll look up the record behind your prints and you'll make the papers. Now—are you going to behave?"

Kerner had made his last effort. He nodded dumbly and when the prowl car arrived, shambled toward it almost drunkenly. Thursday knew the driver and promised to file charges later in the afternoon. The story held up under the casual police questions. Thursday was known and a trickle of blood stained his chin where Kerner had hit him. Kerner, unshaven and pallid and mussed, looked like just another vagrant.

When the prowl car roared off, Thursday found a lonely bench in the terminal and sorted through the blackmail material again. He tore off the flap of the envelope and made himself a list of names. The photo copies ranged from hotel registries and personal letters to candid pictures and one prison record.

But there were no duplicates of ten IOUs from The Natchez bearing the signature of Irene Whitney. Thursday frowned and puzzled and gave up. For some reason, the blonde woman's gambling notes weren't being handled through the usual Night & Day channels.

He rented a safety deposit box in the Coronado branch of the Bank of America under the name of James Donald and left his morning's haul hidden there. He spent another half hour poring through the bank's phone directory, matching numbers with the list of names on the envelope flap. Then he had lunch at a sandwich shop.

The cashier said, "You look like your mother-in-law just died, mister."

"Honey, I have struck uranium in my back yard. Give me a couple dollars' worth of nickels. I want to tell all my friends."

Thursday spent his afternoon, with short breaks for air, closeted in a phone booth. Painstakingly, while sweat dripped onto his brown paper list, he traced every name. To each, his proposition was the same: "I know you are being blackmailed. My office is in a position to recover all material being used against you. Would you care to retain me as your representative at one hundred dollars flat fee? On a contingency basis, of course."

The reaction ran the gamut, ranging from frightened denials of understanding what he was talking about to hopeful enthusiasm. When it was over and he emerged from the booth for the last time, hoarse from talking and aching from confinement. Thursday counted the check marks on his list. He had twenty-three new clients.

Twilight was insinuating darkness across the harbor when he rode back, and the North Island beacon was flashing brighter and brighter. He leaned against the forward rail gazing dreamily where the starry lights of San Diego approached. He figured. Twenty-three times a hundred was twenty-three hundred dollars—for doing what he would have to do anyway for Irene Whitney. It was a happy sum.

But that wasn't why he suddenly laughed aloud. A detail had occurred to him in his dreams, a detail still standing between him and twenty-three extra fees. He had to find the original blackmail material.

Chapter 18

THURSDAY, AUGUST 11, 9:00 P.M.

"Okay, Maxie, I'll come down to twenty which is plenty bighearted." Joaquin Vespasian beamed smugly and rocked his little body on the edge of the flowered divan. "Just because I'd rather see you get this than the cops."

Thursday smiled faintly and sighed and put *Heart of Darkness* away in the bookcase. He thought about how he met such interesting people. He stood in the center of the living room of his duplex and eyed this evening's example, Vespasian, nagging him like a gaudy vulgar elf. Vespasian's tanhaired, tan-skinned head suddenly put Thursday in mind of a small basketball and he idly visioned batting it off its plaid body.

Vespasian said, "Well? Twenty because I like you, Maxie. We can get along." He winked.

Thursday winked back, poker-faced. "Now you've come hinting around, chum, you might as well know you're not leaving without a chat. But I never pay in advance."

"You muscle boys think you can shove anybody around." Vespasian popped some gum in his mouth, sneering discreetly.

"That's right." Thursday sat on the arm of the easy chair by the door, waiting.

"Okay, if that's the way you deal. I'll trust you to pay up because this is going to bowl you over. Monday you were hunting a character by name of J. X. O'Connell." Vespasian lidded his owl eyes. "Maxie, I got him."

"That's very interesting, your work. Monday, I mentioned O'Connell's name and you fell all over yourself volunteering to help me find him. But you didn't bother to ask what he looked like. But you found him anyway. I think I'll call Clapp just to hear him laugh."

"Now don't get your bowels in an uproar. This is how it was." Vespasian chomped his gum and folded his hands around a bony knee. Thursday noticed his cufflinks were shined dazzlingly but the cuffs were limp and soiled. Typical. "Monday I was just keeping the old mind open. If you *had* trusted me with O'Connell's looks, we might have saved some valuable time. You know what I hooked together, Maxie? The papers said a certain well-dressed gent was seen with Papago Monday night. Keeping the old mind open did the rest."

"Okay. Then you know O'Connell."

"Not as O'Connell, you might know. The name he gave me was Fathom, Colonel Ellis Fathom."

Thursday snorted.

"Oh, that Colonel angle's just flash. It just doesn't matter. What's a name? The world the way it is, we can't be choosy about who we meet."

"No, we certainly can't."

"Colonel Fathom," said Vespasian, "lives just three blocks from here, Maxie. He came in at eight forty-five and I ran right down here. Now let's talk payoff in the same language. I put my half straight."

Thursday got up and ambled over to Vespasian. He patted his hands over the plaid suit. No gun. He went back and relaxed in the big chair. "Vespasian, let's talk the same language, period. Out of this fair city—four hundred thousand population—you recognized this Fathom-O'Connell by a one-line description in the papers which said, as I remember, only that he was tall and gray-haired and well-dressed. And after recognizing him from last night's papers, you waited one whole day before coming to see me about it. Keep spinning."

Vespasian only smirked. "You're hashing up my story. Okay, so let me put this tag on it. This Colonel Fathom joe came to see me in connection with George Papago, about two weeks ago. Somebody—now, I don't know who—had told

Fathom that Nell Kopke was a client of mine. He wanted me to milk her for some kind of information. I turned him down."

"Why? Wasn't his money good?"

"Not good enough. In Nell I had a good, steady income sucker. I wasn't going to kick that out the window for a one-shot with this Fathom."

"Uh-huh. So why the hiatus between you knowing who I was after and letting me know?"

"Maxie, you keep forgetting I got a mouth to feed. I figure my dope is worth more to you if I can lay the old finger on Fathom. So it took me twenty-four hours which I call pretty good." Vespasian split his wise face with a grin. "See, I got notions of connecting with your setup in a quiet way. Cops—mostly what I get out of them is certain freedom of operation. A smart fellow like you might mean something more usable to a smart fellow like me. Usable meaning money."

"Before you paint your name on my door," Thursday said dryly, "let's empty the old pockets concerning Fathom."

"All-around boy, if the gossip's right. He's been a sideshow barker, a pitchman, fronted for some con jobs, did some Federal Theater acting way back when. Last local job was some valet deal—ended about a year ago. Of course, he's had stuff going on the side I didn't hear about."

"Valet," said Thursday thoughtfully. He wandered into the bedroom and got his hat and coat. "Let's go round him up, Vespasian. You've sold me."

The little man beamed and winked. "I told you."

They took Vespasian's middle-aged Ford sedan, chugging up the hill toward Balboa Park by way of Laurel Street. It was a neighborhood where weathered frame mansions brooded over squat new stucco houses. Some of the tall old houses still were sprucely kept: most of them sported Rooms—Kitchen Privileges signs and their yards looked tired. Vespasian wheeled up the cracked driveway of one of these and stopped under the ivied porte-cochere. A cold light beamed down on the two men as they slid silently out of the car. Thursday brushed along the head-high evergreen hedge overgrowing that side of the driveway and rounded the sedan to join Vespasian on the porch.

The little man raised his eyebrows, thumbing up at the only lighted window on the second floor. "Check'll do if you don't have cash."

They pushed through the heavy front door and stood in a dim hallway of closed doors and an ornate staircase. A radio audience applauded in some unseen parlor. The smell of years and stale cooking hung in the air. But none of the boarders made an appearance as Vespasian lightly led the way up the carpeted steps.

He stopped without knocking before the first door to the left on the head of the stairs. He grinned gaily and rubbed his hands.

Thursday clamped a hand on Vespasian's shoulder and held him in front of him as a shield. Then he knocked gently. Carpet slippers plopped across wooden flooring toward the door. It opened broadly, unsuspectingly, and for the second time Thursday gazed into the shocked eyes of Colonel Ellis Fathom, alias J. X. O'Connell.

Thursday propelled his shield into the room first and the pseudo Colonel backed away, mouthing incoherence. Thursday shot the bolt and the three were alone in the bedroom.

Fathom scrambled for his dignity and managed a weakly hearty laugh. Steam wisped from the tiny bathroom where he had just bathed and shaved. His pompous face was still pink from the razor. His dressing had gotten no further than a white linen shirt and cobalt silk shorts. He was bravado on skinny legs. "So you've caught up with me, eh?"

Thursday said nothing. Vespasian flitted from between the two tall men and loitered by the scarred bureau. Fathom laughed again, more successfully. "Very clever of you, I concede that. It must have been no small task to ferret me out. You deserve my compliments."

Thursday nodded and began to drift silently around the room. He fingered through the contents of Fathom's trouser pockets, piled neatly on the bureau. The wallet was empty and he stared thoughtfully at Vespasian who relinquished the seventeen dollars in bills he had palmed.

"However, perhaps it's bad form for the hare to compliment the hounds, even such extremely persistent hounds," Fathom said. The elderly man was posturing desperately and there was a keen edge of terror to his cultured voice. Thursday rummaged through the bureau drawers, glancing now and then at Fathom in the mirror but saying nothing.

"Of course, you've not a particle of proof. Not one particle. You may suspect what you please but it will take more than these highhanded tactics to stand up in our courts of law...."

From beneath the undershirts in the bottom drawer, Thursday pulled a box of stationery. Beneath the monogrammed paper was a thin packet of newspaper clippings, held together with a rubber band. Fathom coughed, choked and went on urgently, "I freely admit that I should have come forward when I read of the tragedy but that's a crime of omission. I didn't care for the notoriety, that's all."

When he had finished riffling through the clippings, Thursday tossed them on the bureau. He looked under the mattress of the unmade bed and under the chair cushion. He opened the closet and touched through the pockets of all the suits quickly while Fathom expostulated with growing frenzy behind him. They were beautifully woven, beautifully cut garments that Thursday would have liked to own. The oddity of envy in this situation flicked him piquantly.

He turned away from the closet with a single find. Fathom saw it and his voice died away. It was a lightweight, inexpensive bamboo cane, glistening new.

Flexing the bamboo in both fists, Thursday said softly. "Now tell me about killing George Papago."

Fathom blurted, "I'm an innocent man. The last I saw of Papago was on the night he was killed, yes, but I left him alive. I left him alive and alone with Irene Whitney."

Chapter 19

THURSDAY, AUGUST 11, 9:45 P.M.

The sterling ring of his alibi seemed to give Colonel Fathom courage. He drew erect and smiled smoothly, fingering his crisp mustache. "So you see, Thursday, you've accomplished a very small thing by tracing me through this—" he indicated Vespasian "—grimy Judas. Certainly I knew he was following me today. But such was my confidence—"

Thursday shrugged. "Play it any way you like."

"Furthermore, I'm not aware of any official standing on your part."

"Get your pants on, Colonel, and I'll introduce you to a man who has that."

Fathom chuckled but his eyes shifted. "Really, is there any need to bring the police into this—for no reason? I am absolutely innocent of even complicity in *l'affaire* Papago. I'll admit the circumstances look bad for me. But they look equally bad for you, I would say."

Vespasian looked at Thursday with wily interest. He murmured, "A point I tried to make before, Maxie. Now suppose you let me—"

"Save your friendship for later," Thursday said.

"Circumstances being thus and so," Fathom continued, "I thought you might perhaps care to overlook finding me. In return, I might—well, supply you with the true facts of the case."

"If you're trying to cop a plea—" Thursday idly spun the bamboo cane "—you have the floor."

Fathom cleared his throat, all oratorical confidence. "As you probably know, I was the private representative of a woman named Irene Whitney. She engaged me last week to purchase one-thousand-dollars' worth of gambling chits from this George Papago fellow. They were debts incurred by her before the city seized The Natchez. I paid off those notes with no trouble at all."

"Uh-huh."

"I delivered the chits to Miss Whitney at her penthouse on the John C. Frémont Hotel. She paid me for my labors and I considered the matter closed. Then on Monday evening this strange situation arose. Papago accosted me and accused me of lying to him, cheating him. He demanded to see Miss Whitney. He was a bit muddled with drink but he was so wildly threatening that I eventually gave in and took him to her penthouse."

"Uh-huh."

"It's quite true. That is exactly where I left him, alive and well, if angry. If you're wondering why I haven't been to the authorities with this story, Thursday, put yourself in my boots. I have a slight police record elsewhere and I should have undergone endless inconvenience."

"Uh-huh. Endless. What does this Irene Whitney look like?"

"Oh, a striking woman, thirtyish, black hair like yours, Thursday. Her inclination to flesh doesn't detract from her appeal in the least and she has splendid features, rather oriental." Fathom smiled, man to man. "I dislike compromising a lady with such a revelation as mine, but in the final extremity . . . "

Thursday laughed at him, thinly, and Fathom looked indignantly puzzled. Thursday said, "Well, this is it, the final one. Here's what really happened. The woman you describe is Quincy Day, as if you didn't know. You've worked for her quite a while. One of your assignments was as valet to Perry

Showalter, some time back. You collected the data that your organization was using to blackmail him." He pointed the cane at the bureau, at the packet of newspaper articles. "From all these clippings about Showalter's smashup, I gather you're pretty proud of your work. You even began thinking that you were quite a wheel in said organization. So when Papago tracked you down Monday night, you went ahead and acted on your own instead of calling the boss first. That was a stupid mistake for all concerned."

Fathom's cheeks were less pink and he lost his breath momentarily. Vespasian, without stirring or changing the cocksure lift of his eyebrows, had suddenly repledged his allegiance to the detective.

Thursday went on, "First you found out from Papago that I was meddling in your business. Then you agreed to take him to Quincy. But when Papago took you to his car, he must have said something about mine being parked right in back of him. That did it for George. You slugged him then and there, shoved him into his convertible and threw his bloody hat onto my front seat. Then you hurried back to the bar to phone Quincy and tell her how brainy you'd been."

Hoarsely, Fathom said something that ended. ". . . guesswork!"

"Made to measure, Colonel. Papago had to be dead when you went back to make that phone call. After he spent all evening catching up with you, he'd never have let you out of his sight. I'll bet Quincy really had a catfit when she found what you'd done, didn't she? There were so many simpler ways of dealing with Papago, even to cutting him in. But you couldn't unweave your own idiot answer. So you took Papago out to the alligator farm—or Quincy had one of her staff do it while you pieced together an alibi. The hat was supposed to scare me off and the Papago-alligator publicity was supposed to scare Irene Whitney but—"

"Wait a minute!" cut in Vespasian. His voice squeaked uncertainly. "Maxie, this hat—the one I found—"

"Shut up." Thursday held Fathom's eyes. "You got a better lie handy, Colonel?"

"Maxie, what kind of a frame you trying to—"

"Shut up."

The smile Ellis Fathom tried on was ghastly. "Really, Thursday, I should have you arrested for slander."

Thursday swished the slender cane through the air under the other man's nose. "Bamboo's a talkative wood all of a sudden. You see, you're the first guy of your kind I've ever met who didn't have a weapon handy of some sort—knucks or a sap or even a penknife. This bamboo thing is no weapon, and as a dress accessory it's all wrong. It's too light for a man your size and too cheap to go with your clothes. You used to carry a heavy walking stick but you broke that over Papago's head. It had to be destroyed along with Papago's clothes and wallet with that phony card of yours. But you were used to carrying something so you got this cheap affair. Either you're low on funds or it was your guilt complex or maybe both. Clapp'll find witnesses to prove you carried a potential murder weapon up till Monday night."

The fear graying Fathom's face froze into a mask of unreason. He flung himself forward at his tormentor. Thursday leveled the cane like a rapier and Fathom met the ferrule with his groin. The bamboo bent springily and the half-dressed man doubled on the floor in agony.

Vespasian giggled. "One down," he said.

Thursday looked at him expressionless and tossed the cane on the bed. "Get a suit out of the closet," he ordered. To Fathom: "Anything you want to add, Colonel? Better think in a hurry. Otherwise, you're going to the gas chamber, and through you I'll get Quincy Day."

Fathom did not try to speak. He panted, his face aging and helpless, and he looked around at the doors, which held no escape for him. Thursday and Vespasian had to lift him to his feet and help him slip into trousers and coat.

They didn't bother to change his carpet slippers for shoes.

Thursday shouldered him to the doorway and Vespasian twisted the knob nervously, hesitating. He said, "How about the payoff?"

"Later."

"I want it now. I don't like this always later talk. I dealt fair with you, Maxie, and did nothing but favors. Something's going on I don't like. How did I get rung in on this deal?"

Thursday opened the door and got Fathom into the hall. The man, sunk in dull apathy, let himself be guided. Thursday held his arm in one hand and caught Vespasian's with the other. "Because you belong in."

The little man squirmed as they went down the stairs but couldn't shake loose. "I got nothing to do with this stuff except what I told you. I tried to help you. Now you act like you're taking me in."

"You guessed it."

"No!"

An old man in a smoking jacket peered out the parlor doorway as they passed. Thursday shook Vespasian silent. "You got more to tell, Vespasian. Papago dragged you into this case by accident but you belong in. The hat was the tip-off. An honest man would have taken it directly to the cops. An unimplicated crook, which is what you pretend to be, would have destroyed it and kept shut up. But you brought the hat to me because you knew what was going on and you wanted an excuse to see what I was doing about it. Now you know."

They reached Vespasian's car under the porte-cochere. "Okay, see it my way," the little man was saying. "I'm not scared to tell you there's a couple minor details I haven't exactly been waving around. But strictly—"

"Into the front," Thursday said. "Both of you. I'll sit in back where I can watch."

Fathom slid under the wheel and over to the hedge side. Vespasian argued, "Now, look. There's nothing to gain by spoiling my good name down at headquarters when I can tell you right here and now—"

Thursday lifted him bodily and shoved him behind the wheel and slammed the door on him. He climbed into the back seat and said, "Headquarters."

Vespasian twisted around, pleading. "I didn't spill my guts up till now because I was scared. Listen to me! When Colonel Fathom first came around to my joint—"

The tall hedge on Fathom's side of the sedan exploded in a blast of gunfire.

Thursday found himself sprawled on the cement drive without remembering the instinctive dive for cover. The thunder of the fusillade—somebody had emptied a clip, at least—was only an echo now but tardy splinters of glass still fell about him. He couldn't hear. He felt alone.

But he raised himself cautiously to peer into the car. The front seat was a shambles. Shards of windshield sparkled on Fathom, who had been knocked sideways, his unrecognizable head down behind Vespasian's back. Vespasian lay forward, hugging the steering wheel, while a trickle of blood coursed down his plaid coat and more blood hung a red veil over his face.

Lights were popping on in the boarding house and a door hanged excitedly. Thursday sprinted down the driveway toward a break in the hedge, growling in impotence. He charged into the next yard but it was empty. On the other side of the hedge, where the assassin had waited, a dry branch smoldered from muzzle blast.

Thursday ran toward the garage, crossing into another back yard, searching for some trace. The ground was hard and sunbaked. Two houses away a dog barked—he noticed then his deafness was gone—and he raced in that direction. No one was in sight. Then a woman rattled a back door and yelled something at him.

He vaulted another fence, came out a driveway onto

Kalmia Street. In the distance he could hear the sirens rising and falling. He spun around, irresolute. Then, welcoming shadows, he began walking swiftly down the hill toward his home.

CHAPTER 20

THURSDAY, AUGUST 11, 11:30 P.M.

Austin Clapp dented the flowered divan considerably more than Vespasian had earlier. He regarded Thursday with truculent amusement. "Pajamas, robe, and good book. Where's your faithful dog?"

"He left me to join the force. Going to take off your hat or isn't this a social call?"

Thursday ambled barefoot into the kitchen and poured a beer for his visitor. He heard Clapp glance into the kitchen after him and then into the bedroom but he didn't give notice. When he took the foaming glass in, the homicide chief had his hat off and was stretched lazily along the divan with his feet up on the arm.

"Thanks," Clapp said and gulped off half the beer. "Well, maybe you *don't* know about tonight's new business. Hear the sirens?"

"About an hour ago. They don't thrill me any more."

"You poor kid. These would have. A cowboy-and-Indian ambush just up the hill from you. Remember that immune friend of yours?"

"Vespasian?"

"Right. I should have kept my men on him. He turned out to be not so immune to bullets."

"Dead?"

"Not yet. The docs at County Hospital are flipping coins. He took a slug through the right side of his chest and another across the hairline that bounced off his skull. He bled. But the guy with him—name of Ellis Fathom—couldn't be deader. One through the neck killed him, two more removed his face." Clapp described the car-hedge setup. "Somebody wasn't taking chances."

"Who wasn't? And on what?"

"Very funny," Clapp muttered. "Turn on your radio. The news flashes got as much on it as I have. Fathom lived at this boarding house. One of the other boarders saw him and Vespasian leave together just before the fireworks—along with another man."

Thursday was lighting a cigarette. He was proud of the way his hands were disciplined. "That should be a lead."

"Sure, it should. But you know my luck. My witness is an old gaffer with a cataract in each eye. He's doing fine to be sure there was another man, let alone describe him." Clapp swore pensively and emptied his glass. "Fathom used to be a tall gray-haired fellow, expensive clothes, lived in a dump. That's about all we know."

Thursday knew different. Clapp probably had already linked Fathom with Showalter. There was a *Sentinel* final edition on the floor by the divan; the number two story was Merle Osborn's revelation of Showalter's recent financial collapse, coupled to obvious hints. But the Showalter suicide would be Benedict's pet case and Clapp wasn't airing the D. A.'s secrets.

Clapp said, "Still . . . when you add this Vespasian tout who's also got a finger somewhere in the Papago killing, you—"

"You're thinking Fathom might be the guy who was with Papago in the bar."

"Could be. Don't forget there was another man on that scene, too. But why kill Fathom? To shut him up? Or is it vengeance for Papago?" Clapp shook his head. "That doesn't fit too good. Nell Kopke left town this morning. The railroad detectives saw her off with tickets to Philadelphia for her and her kid. Her furniture was shipped to Philadelphia, too."

"You let her go?"

"She wasn't too material a witness. I can get her back if I need her."

"What was the weapon tonight?"

"A .32 revolver. Keating—ballistics—rode along to collect slugs and he said, at first glance, they were fired through a Colt-type barrel. But that covers a good many makes of guns. I say revolver because we didn't find any ejects scattered around where the killer waited behind the hedge. Nickel-jacketed bullets." Clapp lapsed into pondering.

Thursday thought back. Nell Kopke had carried a .32 Colt revolver. But he remembered the bullets distinctly: ordinary unjacketed lead slugs.

The telephone interrupted. Thursday said, "Excuse me," and went out to the kitchen to answer it.

Quincy Day's voice throbbed low and sweet. "I had to call up to apologize, Max," she said. "I do hope you've forgiven me for my performance yesterday."

He squinted at the receiver in disbelief. "I seldom hold a grudge."

"One of many good facets, I'm certain. Do you ever get feelings about people, Max? I do. I suppose you'll term it silly—most men do—but I find that most of my intuitions are wonderfully accurate. And I must confess to a very very strong feeling about you."

"What about me? You're doing fine."

"I should say about you *and* me. I sense a wrongness in our working against one another. It should be the other way entirely. Please give me the chance to convince you, Max."

"With or without cops this time?"

She chuckled disarmingly. "Then you actually haven't forgiven me yet. I don't really mind. I think I'm stubborn enough to win you over. Why don't we have breakfast together tomorrow?"

"Sure. Where?"

"Don't be foolish, Max. Here, of course. My apartment."

"Eight o'clock sound too eager?"

"Just right." She paused, then chuckled again. "I notice that you didn't inquire where my apartment is. That's a very encouraging sign. Till eight then, darling."

Clapp was still stretched along the divan, carefully inattentive, when Thursday returned. He said, looking up, "Two to one that was your girl Osborn with the poop on the Fathom killing."

"That's what makes a great detective. Intuition."

"I like a man who respects his elders." Clapp caught himself yawning and sat up abruptly. "I better get it off my chest—why I came. This isn't official, just friendly, Max. Two men have been killed, maybe Vespasian will make a third. Benedict is swearing up and down that you're in this show someplace and he intends to nail your hide to the wall if he can. So if you're holding back anything, now is the time to unload while I can still give you a hand. Later, I might not be able to."

Thursday said gently, "Thanks a lot, Clapp. I appreciate it. Matter of fact, I have been thinking similar thoughts all evening. You know how I go for the long chance—but the client I got now is leaving me a little too wide-open. So maybe we ought to drop out and have a session with Benedict."

Clapp got to his feet, grinning. "Now you're talking. I'll ring him while you're getting dressed. He's a health fiend—in bed by nine every night."

They drove through the night to La Mesa in Clapp's sedan, a half-hour ride which sped them by the dark buildings of the Molyneux Alligator Farm. Behind the foothill community, Clapp turned into a long, orchard-flanked road. He muttered, "Wouldn't you know Benedict would have a hundred and forty-five avocado trees, *too*?"

Leslie Benedict opened the front door himself; even in

dressing gown and pajamas he looked as classically imposing as his Georgian house. He led the way to a prim study and settled into a leather chair with cool condescension. Clapp and Thursday found seats for themselves.

"Well, Thursday . . . " The district attorney was struggling to keep the open mind he was proud of, but his yellowish eyes were hostile as he regarded the man who had broken his sleep. "Lieutenant Clapp informs me that you've had a change of heart concerning the Papago case."

"You can put it that way. I put it that it's my duty as a citizen to aid justice wherever possible."

"Which is certainly high-principled of you."

Clapp said, "Let's all of us keep this amiable. Thursday's offering some help. I'm willing to hear about it."

Benedict's short mouth puckered and then said slowly, to no one, "I like to think that I'm a fair man. If I've acquired personal prejudices against a person because of his activities in the last few years, I don't want them to stand in the way of justice. Consider that an apology, Thursday, if you need one." He pressed his fingertips to one eyebrow briefly, massaging that side of his forehead out of shape. "No, I have never looked upon myself as a particular lover of humanity, *in esse*, but I admit I have been disturbed lately. I have been disturbed by a certain brutal significance of recent deaths."

His glance flicked to a copy of the *Sentinel* folded under a paperweight. Uppermost was Merle Osborn's story which made the Showalter scandal public fare. Benedict didn't ask if Thursday was responsible for that disclosure although the thought was on his face. He said, "I'm listening."

Thursday nodded gravely and relaxed in his chair. They were all three on the same team. "This is how I got my foot stuck in the Papago case. Last Monday, at noontime, I met a woman who—"

The study door opened. Benedict was seated facing it and Thursday saw him smile warmly, an expression he had never seen on the man's face before.

Thursday twisted his head around and then rose, with Clapp. A woman stood in the doorway, hesitantly. The skirt of a nightgown floated under the hem of her ruffled blue negligee, pale blue which matched her eyes and emphasized her blonde hair. She said to Benedict, "Excuse me for interrupting, dear, but I thought perhaps you might care for some coffee. I can—"

Her eyes took in Thursday and her clipped voice died away. Her throat tightened, as it had in the house at Loma Portal, where she had called herself Irene Whitney.

Benedict said, "No, thank you, my dear. I'll need my sleep tonight and you know what coffee does to that. Irene—you've met Lieutenant Clapp, and this is Mr. Thursday whom he brought with him. My wife, gentlemen."

Clapp murmured something and Thursday supposed he did, too. Irene Benedict's lips were pale but she spoke again to her husband, managed a blankly gracious smile and backed into the hall, closing the door. As the outer shadows fell across her face, Thursday saw her eyes stab at him with a quick desperate appeal. Then he was looking at a closed door.

"Very well," said Benedict, reseating himself. "You became involved in the Papago case Monday noon."

"Yes," said Thursday. His thoughts spun around, pouring from one to another like a waterwheel. He stalled for time, getting comfortable in the chair and searching his pockets for nothing. Benedict was waiting. Thursday said, "Well, last Monday I was approached by a woman. She asked me to protect a little mind-reading quack named Joaquin Vespasian. Her name was Nell Kopke."

Benedict's face showed no expression whatsoever but Clapp wore a small frown. Thursday continued glibly, "I went out to see Vespasian. From him I learned that Nell Kopke was Papago's mistress and that Papago was jealous of this Vespasian. With good reason, too, I guess. But, anyway, I agreed to keep an eye out—and that same night Papago's bloody hat was left on Vespasian's front doorstep. Naturally, I took the story to Clapp. Right?"

There was a moment of silence. Then Benedict said, "Go on."

Thursday looked surprised. "That's all there is to tell, I strung along with the case after Papago's death, out of loyalty to Nell Kopke. But now I understand that she has left town, and Vespasian has been shot, so I feel that I am violating no confidences in telling you the whole sordid tale." Thursday spread his hands. "So there you are."

A flush spread under the tan egg-shape of Benedict's face and he stood up. He jerked the belt of his robe tighter around his middle. "Do you mean to tell me that I was roused from a warm bed—the second time this evening, thanks to that other killing—to waste my time on your inanities?"

"I'm sorry," said Thursday. "I thought it was pretty unimportant myself but Clapp insisted."

Clapp slammed to his feet. "What's going on here?"

"That is precisely my inquiry," Benedict said icily. "Why you should find it necessary to burden me with these immaterial facts which you are supposedly capable of evaluating for yourself, I fail to see. Frankly, Lieutenant, such behavior argues a deplorable lack of judgment from your department."

"Slow down," Clapp rumbled. "First, let's straighten out a few—"

"Not tonight, please," Benedict cut him off. "I have a full day scheduled tomorrow so if you'll excuse me, gentlemen . . ." He was holding the study door open for them.

Clapp started to say something more, halted to chew his lip angrily and then stamped out of the room. Thursday followed him meekly. The homicide chief hunched over the steering wheel and didn't speak until Thursday got out in front of his duplex.

"Nice hot potato," Clapp growled.

"I'm sorry," Thursday said softly. "I didn't mean to lay it in your lap. When I started analyzing the situation for Benedict, I caught on to something I hadn't thought of before. You know how things suddenly latch together in your mind. And there was a confidence involved which—"

"Never mind your reasons. I suppose you got them but they better be good for your own sake. It's your neck, not mine."

"I hope they're good."

"I don't know what you're out to win with cuteness, but I bet it ends up nothing more than a taste in your mouth. You won't take home any prizes if you keep kicking the law around. Close the door. I got some sleep to get, too."

"Okay. Good night, Clapp."

Clapp didn't answer and the police sedan roared off. Thursday stood on the curb a moment, watching its taillight disappear and leave him alone in the warm night. He felt tired himself. He sighed and went into his house.

He stayed up, smoking and trying to read, until nearly three o'clock. He glanced up from the book quickly once, with the distinct impression that he was surrounded by a sticky web he couldn't quite see. He warmed up the coffee and it was bitter. He waited for a phone call from Irene Benedict but it didn't come.

Chapter 21

FRIDAY, AUGUST 12, 5:30 A.M.

A couple hours of poor sleep and Thursday got up to face Friday. He drove to Mission Beach through a hazy rising sunlight that promised another scorching day.

The little stucco and red-tiled Papago house sat empty,

stale, among the other beach bungalows which were only sleeping to the surf music. Thursday trudged around it, peeping through the curtainless windows at bare floors and walls. He didn't know what he was looking for, only that it seemed necessary this inspection be made. The steel trash barrels in the alley overflowed with moving-day debris and a half-dozen empty whisky bottles were intermingled with the topmost strata. Through the kitchen window, Thursday could see another fifth on the sink, as good as empty, and a tumbler near it with still a rinse of amber liquid coating the bottom.

The trip was a waste of gas except for the peace of driving. He killed some more time lazing his Olds around Mission Bay back to the city. He put the car in the garage of the John C. Frémont Hotel and sat in a corner of the vast marble lobby behind a newspaper, watching the bank of elevators. The *Sentinel* had closed its forms shortly after midnight but there was nothing important about the double shooting that he didn't know—except for the boldface bulletin which said Joaquin Vespasian would live.

At eight o'clock he discarded the newspaper and took an elevator up to Quincy Day's apartment which was not on the hotel roof but three stories beneath.

"You're giving men the wrong impression," he told Quincy as she took his hat.

"Oh, I hope so, that being one of woman's greatest pleasures." A quilted housecoat of white silk covered even her wrists, pretending demureness as it flowed down over her obvious figure. Less demure was the zipper track shooting from throat to ankle. She had forsaken her harlequin glasses and high heels; her canted eyes were on a level with his mouth. She stood quite still for the moment, smiling slightly and letting herself be seen against her decor. Thursday thought, the witch at home, and found himself enjoying her presence once more against his better judgment. It was as if the idea of her probable wickedness were a joke for them both to laugh at, and any crimes she might commit merely prankish white magic. Quincy let the stiff, period formality of her apartment frame her exotic head in contrast and then, having had her pose, she raised her eyebrows like batwings. "But what specific instance might you have in mind, Max? The rather impolite curtain I rang down on our last encounter? I'm really—"

"No, Fathom said this place was a penthouse."

"People are so limited in their vocabularies, aren't they?" She linked his arm in hers with an innocent friendliness he found difficult to doubt. "Come along and I'll show you what he meant." But her quilted silk hissed against his coat sleeve in warning.

They crossed the Persian rug of the square, haughty living room to french doors, already open onto a small terrace of red cement. A low wall guarded the sheer drop to Broadway and enclosed tiny hedged flowerbeds and four potted fan palms. Above loomed three more floors of hotel and a blue-white sky.

"The management calls it a terrace garden apartment on the bill, I believe. There are only six of them and I had to wait forever on a list to get this one. During the war they all went to generals or admirals or deities at Consolidated—but now it's mine. How do you like it, Max?" She chuckled gaily. "At the first of my occupancy, I completely forgot those windows above until the manager suggested—with the most delicate of coughs—that perhaps the hotel could furnish me a sunlamp if I were really so intent on a tan. Somebody had complained."

Thursday started to say that he wouldn't but she swung onto the subject of breakfast. "I thought we might have it out here. It's perfect in the morning, especially this morning. I abhor going to work. About ten it commences getting hot, though, or I probably never would get to the office and shoulder my burden. Give me your coat. I'm going to put you to work. Besides, I think it's foolish to be dressed at breakfast, especially in California. Back east, there's some excuse for coats, but not here. I trust you can wrestle that table outside, and the cloth and silver are in the hall closet."

He handed over his coat and grinned. "Now, can I say something, Quincy?"

"Oh, dear, have I been babbling again? Don't tell me you're going to seek refuge in a hurt I-am-company attitude which I think is—"

"What part of back east you from?"

"Can our kind of person say we come from any one particular place and have it mean anything?"

"Maybe your kind can't. My kind is a local product, traveled at government expense and came home to stay. Why'd *you leave* home?"

"Now, Max..."

She bounced out to the kitchenette and began rattling things. Thursday moved the Queen Anne tea table onto the terrace and set it. Later, he lounged in the kitchenette doorway and watched what she put into the breakfast.

Quincy turned around, skillet in hand, smiling. "Did you give the place a good searching, darling?"

"Uh-huh. Looked pretty normal. I find most bedrooms equipped with photographers these days."

She laughed. "Poor Max! I wish I'd known you better then. So much effort and general untidiness could have been avoided—not that I'm admitting anything, understand. How do you like your eggs?"

"Fresh and many. Fathom died a pretty untidy death."

"Business at this hour? I consider three eggs many."

"Three's fine. Vespasian didn't look so hot either. Going to try again?"

"I *can* spare four. But there's lots else."

"No, three's fine."

He helped her carry the plates to the terrace. He had arranged his chair so he could watch the french doors and the tiers of windows above. There was nothing to watch, the food was good, and Quincy was close and companionable across the little table. He caught himself relaxing warmly under her stream of conversation. She chatted about nothing sincerely and deftly, while her violet eyes frankly tried to make friends.

She asked him why he didn't take off his necktie since it was so uncomfortable-looking, and he found himself obeying.

Then Thursday smiled quizzically. "I just figured out about you."

"Not business," she begged, pouring coffe.

"Just the opposite—your appeal. Ever since I cornered you in your office, I've been wondering why I should like anything about you. Now, don't interrupt for a change, Quincy."

"Yes, sir."

"Your act is to be a wife. It's in your voice and everything you do. You're good-looking but not so beautiful that you're out of sight. Your appeal isn't sex, at least not in one hammer blow like other women that have your—well, vitality. You spread yours out, surround the object."

"Like a spider? Max, I hate spiders! But tell me more."

"More like quicksand. I understand that's very restful, once you let yourself go. That's your weapon—that illusion of comfort. The idea that you'll be around forever. What adds the spice is that anybody can tell the whole effect is a wonderful lie. You're ready to vanish."

She smiled complacently over her cup. "Most of that was very nice, Max, and I thank you. Your coffee's getting cold, though."

"Yeah." He twined the necktie around his fist and wadded it into his pocket and had a drink of coffee. He added thoughtfully, "It's a shame to destroy a work of art like you. Which I will."

Quincy stuck out her tongue quickly and shrugged. "Oh, well. A shame we should have to give battle when we're so much alike, both adventurers with our own secret Hoyles. Maybe I'm wifely to you because I feel sure of you, darling. I've made it a point to find out what you are and how you operate. You're not narcotized by any of the common mores, nor am I. If you were, I wouldn't be interested in you. For heaven's sake, smile."

"All right. This interest professional or social?"

She set down her cup distastefully. "I should have had better sense than to serve coffee on a day like this. It's so warm." Quincy looked up, her smile wholly unconnubial. "Zip!" she said and pulled the fastener over her bosom to the waist of housecoat. Then she widened her eyes, pretending amazement at her temerity.

Thursday chuckled. "Solely for purposes of ventilation, of course. Cigarette?"

"Ventilation—of course. Cigarette—no, I don't smoke."

He gazed at her through his first puff of smoke and then blew out his match. The flame had quivered more than he cared to admit. "Okay," he said pointlessly.

Quincy leaned her chin on her clasped hands and let her eyes wander over his face. The quilted silk had opened a pathway less than a quarter-inch wide to her middle, more discreet than an evening gown. But the aperture allowed hints of her ivory skin the entire distance, with no lacy interruption by any undergarment.

Their mutual silence had acquired faintly the aspect of a duel when Quincy arose suddenly. "Since you're so helpful, let's clear up the table before we doze off."

They carried the dirty dishes into the kitchenette. Thursday avoided brushing against her rounded body, and she smiled delicately when she noticed. The next time they passed, she swung in a wide circle beyond him, murmuring gravely, "We're electric." She stacked the plates neatly, rinsed her hands and came to where he lingered in the doorway. "Well?"

He asked, "Still too early to discuss business?"

"Oh, much too early."

He pulled the necktie from his pocket and draped it around his neck.

"Don't." Quincy said and pulled it off again. She slid a

plump arm around his waist and leaned her sleek head on his chest. "I'm so bloody lonesome."

"So am I," he muttered.

"Why?"

"You've infected me. You've put yourself across, Quincy. I'm conscious of your position, the way you've got your life jammed crossways in the works. I guess I'm lonesome because I'm going to miss you afterwards."

"I trust *you*."

"Don't be silly. Business is business and I got mine all cut out."

She rose on tiptoe because he wouldn't bend his head. Her mouth covered his gently. Afterwards, she said, "Why did you come? You didn't have to. Was it just business?"

"That's what I told myself."

Quincy chuckled. "I knew better. I knew it in the office Wednesday. I knew you were all trouble and a mile wide." She took her arm away and came around to stand in front of him, apart "Kiss me, trouble."

This time he bent his head and tugged her close. The housecoat gaped. Quincy sighed and stayed against him. "Max, did you like the breakfast? Are you glad you came instead of doing the smart thing? Oh, never mind." She rubbed her hair against his cheek. "I talk too much. I know I do. Don't let me talk."

"Won't they miss you at the office?"

"I told them I wouldn't be in. I tell you I felt sure of you, darling. Try trusting me, just for a little while."

Thursday slowly loosed her arms from his neck. He crossed to the door of her apartment and fastened the night chain. Then he shoved the sofa—it was a Chippendale—across the doorway. He turned to face her across the living room. "When I was a kid, I caught a rattlesnake down our canyon and kept it alive for six weeks. I was crazy about it, and it nearly broke my heart the morning I found it dead. But I never trusted it."

Quincy finished unbuttoning the cuffs of her housecoat. She held out her arms to him, her face dreaming, and whispered. "Now *you're* talking too much."

CHAPTER 22

FRIDAY, AUGUST 12, 4:30 P.M.

Quincy slept deeply while Thursday searched her bedroom. He kept an eye on her or on her reflection in the chiffonier mirror, while he prowled on bare feet. He found her key ring in one of a dozen purses arranged in a closet drawer. He took another look at what he could see of her in the canopied bed—a bare shoulder, a wild tangle of black hair—before he shut himself in the bathroom with the keys. She hadn't stirred.

He softened a cake of soap and made impressions of all five keys. He wrapped the soap in tissue and padded through the bedroom to the hall closet and dropped it in his coat pocket. After replacing her cleaned keys in the purse drawer, he investigated drawers and cupboards in the rest of the apartment. He found nothing he could make important, including the gun.

It was a pearl-handled .32 Colt automatic, in a box in the broom closet. From its oily cared-for condition, he learned that Quincy evidently knew about firearms. The clip was full and the weapon showed no indication of recent firing. Thursday memorized its number and let it go at that since, according to Clapp, a revolver had killed Fathom.

Thursday roamed back to the bedroom. Quincy was still dead to the world, coiled on her right side, both hands under the pillow. He sighed and went to take a shower because he felt grubby. The needle spray didn't wash off the way he felt.

Fingering through the medicine cabinet, he found a half-full bottle of shaving lotion, a shaving mug, a straight razor. Thursday was a little surprised. Quincy's apartment resembled a period exhibit in a museum, and this was the first sign he had discovered of a man's occupancy. He felt strangely better; somehow this transferred part of the trespass from his shoulders to hers.

He carried the shaving equipment into the bedroom and arrayed it on a chair where she could see it when she turned over. Then he got dressed.

He was knotting his tie when Quincy said sleepily, "Good morning, trouble." She was watching him from a little cave under the satin coverlet.

"Afternoon, trouble. It's nearly five."

"Clock watcher. Come over here."

He did. After a while, she chuckled and stretched. "I must look a first-class muddle. My brush and comb are on the dressing table, darling." When Thursday came back with them, she was sitting up, smiling ruefully at the shaving utensils on the chair. "I see you found my brother's things."

They both laughed. Thursday said, "I'm an only child myself. But I make friends easily."

"I'll bet you do, at that." She stopped combing to slap his cheek lightly. "Something so infuriating about that granite expression of yours would make any woman want to use dynamite. Simply to prove you have a human core."

"You found out."

"Did I? I don't know. I suspect you're not human, really, although probably enough for most of the fools. I think I see you because I'm somewhat like you, Max, constantly thinking of three things at once. For instance, what are you thinking about now—besides my unholy beauty, I mean?"

"It's been a long time since breakfast."

"Well, that's a human enough answer, I guess. And you do have a lean and hungry look. Woman's work is never done."

Quincy swung her legs out of bed and slipped into the quilted housecoat. "Why are you so thin, darling? Do you have a high metabolism rate or what?"

"All my rates are high, sweetheart."

"I'm rather famine-struck myself." She kissed him, gathered up the shaving articles from the chair and trotted into the bathroom to put them away again. Thursday listened to her shower for a few minutes and then ambled into the living room. He moved the sofa from in front of the hall doorway. He had a contemplative cigarette—his last one—on the red terrace. The fan palms rustled in a harbor breeze and the shadow of the office building across Broadway lay over the terrace like a mock twilight. Below, a brook of traffic hummed lazily by. He smoked and came near to being at peace . . . but there were the circumstances.

Quincy called from the kitchenette, "Come out and talk to me. I miss you."

He flipped his cigarette into the abyss and went to her. They met over the ringing phone in the living room. Quincy muttered, "Oh, darn!" as she lifted it. She listened, frowning, and said wearily, "Yes, dear. I suppose so. Oh, when you come bring a loaf of bread and a can of coffee. Regular grind."

She returned to her kitchenette, mouth sulky. Thursday said. "Company?"

"Yes." Quincy didn't look around from the spice shelf. "At least, I do have him trained to call in advance."

She wasn't going to discuss it so Thursday simply waited for the unknown *him*, a man to match up with the shaving equipment he had found in the medicine chest.

It was Rupert who, without knocking, used his key on the hall door and opened it to the length of the night chain. His gray-suited keg of body bumped to a halt at the obstacle. His fat, hopeless face showed first mild surprise and then mild foolishness. He said, "I can't get in."

Thursday closed the door, detached the chain and let him enter completely. The short man had an evening paper under his arm and carried a sack of groceries. Quincy came in impatiently. "That was quick, I must say." She bent her cheek for Rupert's kiss and took the groceries in one gesture. "I should have told you to bring cigarettes, too. For Max."

Rupert offered to go down and get some.

"Never mind now. Dinner will be ready right away." Quincy swept back to her kitchenette.

The two men glanced at each other. Thursday felt embarrassed. Rupert, who apparently didn't, tentatively extended the newspaper. "Care to see the news, Mr. Thursday?"

"Thanks." Thursday sat down in the wing chair and rustled through the pages. No developments in the Papago-Fathom killings had been released, if any. Rupert disappeared into the bedroom and when he returned he had discarded his coat and unbuttoned his vest. He sat down in another chair and folded his hands over his belly, gazing at a corner where no one was likely to appear. He was trying not to disturb anybody.

Thursday read for a while with his eyes only.

Quincy called, "Rupert—I distinctly told you regular grind. Why don't you ever learn anything?"

"They didn't have anything else, dear," Rupert said. "I didn't think it would make that much difference."

Quincy's reply didn't carry into them. Thursday's collar was feeling tight so he loosened his tie. He found himself rereading a story about a dog which had awakened, in the nick of time, its owners in a burning house. He flung the paper aside and stared at Rupert. Rupert awaited his words politely. Thursday forgot what he was going to say when it occurred to him that he had been hogging the entire paper. Before he could make the offer, dinner came.

Quincy served them some casserole dish and a tossed green salad on separate wooden trays. They ate and Quincy did most of the talking, addressing Thursday often as "darling" and almost completely ignoring Rupert. The fat man listened attentively to her, smiled when the subject called for a smile and remained unperturbed. The single reference to Night & Day was Quincy's inquiring, "Did things go well at the office?" and Rupert's answering, "Just an average day."

Finally, the ordeal was over. Thursday carried his tray out and returned with his hat. Quincy sprang to her feet in alarm. "Oh, you're not going! The sun isn't even down."

"Wonderful dinner, Quincy. Wonderful day between meals. But I don't want to interrupt your household routine any more than necessary."

"Now don't start being absurd, darling." Her arm crept around his waist and she rubbed her cheek against his shoulder. "Rupert doesn't mind, do you, dear? Besides, he's no doubt going out somewhere himself, to a show perhaps. He often does after dinner."

Her eyes darted at Rupert and he scrambled up obediently. "Certainly. I intended going to the movies or something."

Thursday snapped, "Why?"

Nobody answered.

"Why? Why don't you tell me to get out of here, Rupert, like any normal man would? Just tell me and there won't be any fuss—I wouldn't have the guts to stay."

Rupert flushed and looked at his pudgy hands before he hung them on his vest pockets. "I don't know what you mean, Mr. Thursday," he murmured.

Quincy said, "You mustn't go, Max, not when we have so much yet to talk about."

Thursday shook his head no, a little helplessly. What got him was the unnatural normalcy of the pair: they couldn't see anything was wrong. A sick wondering about himself tightened like muscle over his undigested dinner. They couldn't see anything was wrong and he was beginning to feel like one of them. He untwined Quincy's embrace and said, "No, I'd rather go. Goodbye, Quincy."

She said, puzzled, "Just goodbye. Is that all?"

Somebody knocked hesitantly. The woman's eyes darkened suddenly. She jerked her head at Rupert who walked slowly to the door and opened it.

Irene Benedict looked in uncertainly at Rupert. Her patrician face smoothed as she saw Thursday and she walked in to him. "Hello," she said. "I'm so glad I finally found you, Mr. Thursday. I've been by your office twice and phoned several times."

"How'd you run me down here?"

She recited her piece. "I had a late appointment downstairs for a permanent. I saw your car in the garage, near mine. One of the elevator boys remembered bringing you to this floor. I've been inquiring in all the apartments."

"That boy's got a long memory." Thursday smiled coldly. "And you're quite a detective yourself."

Irene looked around at Rupert, then at Quincy. When she looked at Quincy she automatically touched back the crinkly blondeness of her new permanent, and her small trim body seemed to twist to a more becoming position within its sea-green rayon. Her face made the same maneuver, putting on a charming smile for the hostess. "I'm awfully sorry, breaking in like this," Irene said. "But I've been anxious to see Mr. Thursday all day and I'm afraid I forgot my manners. I'm Irene Whitney."

Quincy pressed her housecoat over her hips as if welcoming comparison and crooned sweetly. "Oh, no, that's perfectly all right, Miss Whitney. Please don't feel compelled to apologize."

Irene stiffened and the dignified charm froze on her face. Her smile was still fixed flatly as she turned back to Thursday. The words came out between her teeth, "You cheap contemptible crook," and her hand whipped across his cheek.

The slap mark was stinging and Thursday had automatically backed up a pace before understanding set in.

By that time, Irene had whirled on Quincy. "I can hear that

voice even in my sleep," she whispered fiercely. "You're the one, aren't you? The one on the phone!"

Irene went at her, and Quincy was taken by surprise, too. She went over backward, trying to keep her face clear of the raking fingernails, and her head slammed down on one arm of the Chippendale sofa. Irene pounced on top of her, sobbing.

Rupert cried, "Quincy!" and started across the room. Thursday grabbed his arm and took him back to a chair. He sat him down and growled, "We're going to keep out of this one." He anchored the fat shoulder where he wanted it and rubbed the hot place on his cheek with his free hand. They watched.

The fight was swift and vicious. Irene's righteous anger was no match for Quincy Day's experience. They clawed in each other's hair but Quincy used her head to ram at the blonde's face. When Irene's grip was loosened, the other woman began working scientifically with knees and talons. Then Irene's tear-wet face was on the bottom of the tangle, contorted as it probably had not been since childhood.

Thursday said, "Okay. Time." Quincy was sprawled all over the smaller woman, taking her anger out on the green bolero frock. Thursday jerked her to her feet and put her aside. The black hair was spilled about her shoulders but Quincy looked unhurt. She grinned at him with her teeth and commenced fixing her hair.

He helped Irene Benedict get up and he had to support her a minute while she stopped crying. She was a mess. Scratches oozed a mixture with her tears on one cheek, and her other eye was swelling. Her nylons were shredded and she had lost a shoe and her skirt was ripped up one thigh. She clumsily commenced to repair her hair, too, as her first gesture, before she discovered that she had to use both hands on her bolero jacket to be wearing anything above her waist.

The two women glared at each other in the wall mirror

Quincy was using, and there was no sound except for their labored breathing and Irene's hiccuped attempts to control her sobs. Thursday hunted around for the missing shoe and found it and put it on her foot after discarding the remains of that stocking. Then he inspected his client and sighed.

He nodded at Quincy and Rupert and led Irene out into the hall, wondering if the retentive elevator boy would ever forget his departure.

Chapter 23

FRIDAY, AUGUST 12, 7:45 P.M.

Thursday drove his Oldsmobile out Harbor Drive at a conversational speed, but they had crossed the National City line before either of them spoke. He said, "After we've had our talk, I'll take you back to your car. On your way home, I'd advise you to run into a telephone pole at about ten miles an hour. Just enough to bend the bumper and explain that face of yours. You banged it against the steering wheel. There's no story good enough to account for those peekaboo clothes, so you better sneak in quietly. Feeling better now?"

"Yes, much better, thank you." Irene's head lay back against the seat, letting the evening breeze cool her face. "I think there's a coat in the garage I can use." A blush commenced tingeing her cheeks but she didn't open her eyes to inquire, "Am I still decent?"

"Uh-huh."

"Good. I'm so tired." After he'd turned down another suburban street, Thursday glanced at her. The scratches weren't so vicious now that they had dried but the dark eye gave her face a ludicrous lopsided look. She had restored some order to her permanent but the bolero dress Quincy had deliberately vandalized was all through as a garment. A drugstore packet of safety pins had helped; however, her shoulder gleamed beneath one treacherous rip and the green rayon wouldn't stay together over her bare knee.

Thursday said, "Let's clear up a few things. Like why I didn't cancel that catfight as soon as you started fighting. First place, you didn't hire me as a bodyguard. Second place, I was childishly pleased to see you get a lesson knocked into you. You're my client, not my kid sister, and I don't like clients fouling up my plans. Okay, let's hear from you."

"I'm very sorry. For saying what I did and for striking you. But when she spoke in that silky voice. . . . No, I'm not excusing myself because I should have had better control. I'm very ashamed."

"That's over and done. What I meant I want to hear are a few whys and wherefores about this tangle you're in."

Irene opened her eyes and turned her head to stare out at the palm trees marching along the dark avenue. Her words, slow, but chopped neatly by her accent, floated over to him. "The tangle is nearly over and done, isn't that it, Max? I can feel it drawing tighter all the time. She said next week would be the end."

"Suppose you start from the beginning."

She revolved her wedding ring but didn't look at it. "We've been married six years. Try to understand that I don't want to appear disloyal to Leslie, no matter what I may say. This is very difficult to explain."

"Do you love your husband?"

"Why, of course." Irene was surprised. "I've never thought—of course, I do. The root of the thing is my own lack of stability, that's all. Leslie isn't a warm person—I don't mean he isn't fine and thoughtful—but he is so absorbed in his work. I'm glad he has important work. He has that. Perhaps if I had children to keep me busy, I'd—well, I don't and so . . ." She sat up to fumble in her purse. She produced a folded rectangle of brown leather, its design crudely tooled, half of its edges yet to be laced. "So I go to leather-working class and other worthwhile projects. That's where I'm supposed to be right now. I'm making this wallet for Leslie. Don't bother to say how nice it is because I know it isn't. It's botched. I'm not even any good at this."

"He'll be sure to like it, Irene."

"Certainly, he'll say how nice it is and probably treasure it. But we'll both understand that it's poor and useless. Oh, Max, I feel so utterly incapable! I want to be part of something, something that's alive."

"So that's why you started gambling at The Natchez?"

"Yes. I suppose it was a sort of revolt. The losing the money didn't matter. It was even exciting being in debt. It was exciting just *doing* something except club meetings and teas and leather-working class." Irene slid her hands up over her face. She didn't cry and when she folded her hands in her lap again, she said calmly, "You asked me something about Yvonne Odler. I know her slightly and don't like her. But she keeps calling me, wanting me to join some sort of private art class."

Thursday snorted. "You keep saying no. That's definite professional advice at no extra charge. Tell me the rest of it."

"Where are you driving, by the way?"

They had swung onto a deserted hilly road that meandered through the back country. "Taking the long way round to a friend's house. Tell me the rest of it."

Irene contemplated the black asphalt ahead. "I gambled under my maiden name—Whitney. I didn't think about the real risk involved until the morning I read that Leslie had raided The Natchez, closed it up. Then it began to strike home, what an idiot I'd been. Max, I was petrified. First, it was because I thought what an awful scandal there would have been had I been caught in the raid. I didn't even remember the IOUs until quite a bit later. Then I didn't dare to get in touch with Mr. Papago so I let myself hope they had been destroyed. Some papers were, you know. So I didn't do anything at all."

"Papago evidently rescued some of his assets. And evidently Quincy Day already had an eye on your notes from her corner of the web. She bought them up and got to work."

"The evening she telephoned was the most horrible of my life. I never did go to sleep. I sat in bed with my bottle of sleeping tablets, holding them, counting them, actually thinking of taking all of them. But . . . I didn't have the nerve when it came right down to it."

"That's a great definition of nerve: bequeath your husband two black marks for the price of one."

"I'm sorry. I know better. But I've thought since there's a contagion to something so foul. I was trapped and I had to defeat that voice on the telephone, even to using a worse weapon than hers. If I had been able to kill her tonight—" Irene shuddered. She moved closer to him so her shoulder touched his side. The plaintiveness lay implicit in her touch rather than her voice. "Can one's moral senses be dulled, perverted—just by contact, I mean?"

Thursday grimaced. "I wish I knew. I'm sorry myself, for badgering you." He felt her flinch at his harsh chuckle but she stayed pressed against him. "Anybody that makes loud noises about ethics like I do isn't any paragon, you can bet. So Quincy thought she had a string on the D.A., huh?"

"Yes, that's what I couldn't tell you before you found out who Irene Whitney was. That woman actually believed I could persuade Leslie to give up his investigation of the Showalter—" she glanced up at him swiftly "—suicide. It was a suicide, you know. For the same reason as mine would have been."

"I knew already."

"If Leslie didn't bury the case shortly, she promised to publish my IOUs. Which, of course, would cripple Leslie's career. As a figure of justice he would become a laughing-stock, his own wife frequenting those places he's sworn to stamp out.

But what that woman could never understand is that Leslie would never agree to subvert justice even if I should ask him. Even if it meant the end of all his ambitions. You see, he's honest. Implacably honest. She couldn't understand that. She laughed."

"Yeah, she would. Quincy's a lousy judge of character. Most crooks are. They understand weakness—that's their business—but strength is way out of their grasp."

Irene said, "So I called you Monday, after arranging that silliness in Loma Portal, trying to conceal my identity in every way. I hoped you would know a way out—even an illegal way—without harming Leslie. He had spoken of you often."

"I can guess how."

"Yes." She flushed, rattling off quickly, "Let me say here that I no longer agree with him in all particulars. Before I called you I had gone to Leslie's office when I knew he'd be out and pretended to wait for him. I read through all his file on you. That's how I recognized your car in the hotel garage today. There was nothing in the file to—well, to give me any idea you weren't . . ."

"No, your husband isn't in my fan club. Don't worry about it. You hired me and I took you, despite your case, because I liked your looks. I guessed right, about you being an honest woman in a mess. I guessed wrong about you being a good risk."

"So wrong," she said hopelessly. "Next week she'll know I haven't—"

"I don't think so. Quincy already knows you're not cooperating. But blackmail's a bluff so she'll keep hoping, keep calling you. You keep kidding her along." Thursday paused, then went on thoughtfully. "No, our deadline comes when your husband gets hot on her trail. Then she'll realize there's no more chance to buy him off and she'll publish your IOUs out of spite. And also to make him look bad."

"Is that true? That we have more time?"

"All depends. Now I understand why the alligators. Quincy wasn't after press notices so much as she was show-

136

ing off her strength to you—flaunting Papago's body by making a gaudy display practically on your doorstep."

"I suppose. We do live quite nearby, and that's the road I always take home. I slowed down to look last Tuesday afternoon because I saw Leslie's car parked at the alligator farm. But I didn't learn about Mr. Papago until dinnertime."

"I believe you. Has Benedict gotten anywhere on the Showalter case?"

"I don't know. He's pleased about something but he doesn't discuss details with me. I don't imagine that helps. But—"

"Okay. Don't mean to ask you to spy on your husband." Thursday turned the Olds off the pavement onto a rutty filling station driveway. They bounced to a stop beneath the overhang and by gasoline pumps that had been slingshot targets for years. Gardens on both sides nourished sagebrush. The ugly box that had been the station office seemed to rust a little more before their eyes. But a dim light glowed in the tiny frame house fastened behind the derelict.

"Where are we?"

"The friend's," Thursday went around to open her door. She didn't want to go in looking as she did, nor did she want to remain alone in the car. She finally accepted his coat to button around her, and he rattled the sliding iron door of the front building.

Presently, a flashlight played over them from inside the shattered panes. A husky voice swore pleasantly and said, "It's the middle of the night, Max. What you been doing to that poor girl?" The door clanked open.

"None of your business, Coffee, and it's just past nine. This job won't take long."

Coffee blew his nose while his unseen eyes studied Irene. "She'll catch pneumonia," he said and led them through the defunct filling station into the lighted cottage behind. He was a gray, dour little man in overalls and badly fitting teeth which sneered.

There were no introductions. Thursday dug the tissue

wrapped cake of soap from his pocket and handed it to the older man. "Keys. Five of them."

Coffee inspected the soap impressions. "Too close together. Don't you ever learn, Max? I'll do what I can since you're so earnest. Say, thirty minutes."

"Say ten. I don't want to keep you up."

Coffee honked again into his handkerchief—it was silk, in frays—and left the room. His shoes made no noise on the floor. After a moment, the low-pitched whine of a milling machine commenced in a rear room. Irene, sunk in a weedy overstuffed chair by the window, was sniffing with her eyes at the rest of the forlorn furniture and the stained wallpaper.

Thursday said, "Yeah, this is how the other half lives."

"Am I that obvious?"

"You'll admit it's not much like the Benedict manor house and avocado ranch."

"Who is he, Max?"

"Used to be one of the slickest safecrackers in the business. Despite this shack, Coffee has spent more money than you or I may ever see. But his heart went back on him, and he decided another stretch in prison would kill him. Smart man. Not many know when to quit."

"What does he do now?"

"Odd jobs. He's a skilled machinist. I use him every so often. Your husband has a hunch other people do too, but he hasn't been able to prove it."

Thursday turned suddenly and picked up the phone, the only shiny object in the room. "I better get back in touch," he half-explained to Irene as he dialed. The Telephone Secretarial Service had seven calls listed for him: four from a Miss Whitney, two from a Mr. Meier late that afternoon, one from a Miss Osborn at five o'clock. Thursday rang Merle Osborn's desk at the *Sentinel* but she wasn't in.

Next he called the home of John D. Meier who answered still chewing his dinner. "Where you been? I called you twice."

"So I heard. What you got, John?"

"Notes. Wait till I find them." He left the telephone and came back with paper rustling. "You owe me for a long distance call, incidentally. Here's a lady and a case that comes close to your specifications."

"You'll get your money. Give."

"Cleveland, 1942. A wench named Hilda Graves tried a public-carrier accident fraud. She had the help of some faked X-ray plates plus some testimony by a Dr. Theodore Newman. So Newman goes to prison and Hilda got off. It was a male jury. Sex emerged triumphant. Ain't it wonderful?"

"Good boy. Where's Hilda now?"

"I thought you knew. Cross index lost her when she kissed her patsy goodbye at the jailhouse door. How about some handball tomorrow?"

"Let's make it next week. Thanks a million, John. My best to your wife."

A moment's thought and Thursday looked up the number of County Hospital and tried for news of Joaquin Vespasian.

The hospital switchboard girl said, "Just a minute, please," then he could hear muffled voices in the background. The switchboard girl said, stilted, "Mr. Vespasian has checked out, sir. Who—"

"*Checked out?*"

"Mr. Vespasian checked out this afternoon. Who is this calling, please?"

"But he was wounded pretty seriously. He was under police guard."

"I'm afraid I'll have to refer you to the night supervisor, sir. What is your name, please?"

Thursday hung up in a hurry and tried to figure that one out.

Irene Benedict, huddled inside his coat, was gazing out the black window, her fine face upturned and rapt. "There's a shooting star," she murmured. "When I was a child—"

He laughed. "We better take up wishing again. Wish me luck."

Chapter 25

SATURDAY, AUGUST 13, 12:30 A.M.

Feet apart on the soft hall carpet, he stood and considered the door to Quincy Day's terrace apartment. The door, blankly supercilious, absorbed and halted his distrustful gaze.

Thursday tried its brass knob. It was unlocked and he let it glide away from him into a beyond which was unlighted. He stayed out of the aperture it left. Only a little of the hall light entered.

Then he smelled the gas, a smell he could almost see pinching his nostrils. He held his breath where it was and went in, closing the door behind him, striding quickly toward the dim shape of the french doors. He hurriedly opened them wide and stepped out on the terrace for a new lungful of air.

Immediately he left the open glowing night-dark for the doubly smothering dark of the apartment. He jostled period pieces in his hasty prowl to the kitchenette and the hissing rose louder in his ears.

He slapped on the overhead light and twisted off the oven burner of the spotless little stove. The oven door was open, a shelf under Quincy's upper body. Her head was within the enameled cavern, her cheek on a wire grate. Her full body, limply in a praying position, was clad in red lounging pajamas of heavy silk.

The jacket was fastened diagonally across the front by gold monkey heads with rhinestone eyes. Thursday angrily wondered why his mind should be caught up by those when he had enough to do coughing the cloying air out of his chest and hoisting the dead weight of the woman into his arms.

He stumbled back into the living room with her, dropped her on the Chippendale sofa, used the sofa as a pushcart to trundle her into the broad welcome opening of the french doors, found the living room lights and returned, through the brightness which seemed to dissipate the gas, to her body. Quincy was still breathing.

Thursday rolled her over on her stomach and knelt beside her, his big hands deepening the labor of her diaphragm. Her flesh was no less silky than her pajamas under his grasp. At the top of her neck, just below where her black hair swept up into combs, her white skin was insulted by the blue mottling of a bruise.

Quincy gasped out a senseless little cry and tried to raise her head. She hadn't yet opened her eyes. He left her vague stirrings and went back to the kitchenette where the last traces of gas still stung his throat. From a cupboard of bottles, Thursday selected the scotch and a double-ended jigger.

"Here, Quincy. Drink this." In his absence she had gotten over on her back and her eyes of bottomless black stared at the ceiling as if it were falling. The eyes rolled toward him now and took on a reasonable depth. He angled a sofa cushion under her head and tipped a jigger of whisky into her mouth. She strangled, came out of it, and he poured a second down her.

A long way off, her voice said, "Max. Thank you."

"Have another. Make you feel better."

"Lock the door."

He did. When he came back to the sofa, she had inclined herself a little higher on the cushion. She bent her knees so he could sit down with her.

Quincy's eyes were lightening to a more normal purple. Her lips trembled up into a smile, scarlet against her pale, cold-looking face. "I still can't think. Oh, darling, you're wonderful. I didn't know what to do. What's that smell?"

"Your next month's gas bill."

"Was—" She tried to think about it, and her hands were automatically busy arranging her pajama jacket so it covered her stomach. She shook her head, uncomprehending, then winced and felt the back of her neck. "Oh, yes," she whispered. She suddenly spun around so she could lean back across his knees and cling to him, her face against his chest. He put his arms around her shaking shoulders and he held her that way for some time, until she said, "I'm all right." She slid up so her cheek brushed his, and their eyes and mouths were warmly close. "Darling," she said.

Thursday patted her gently. "Suppose you tell me about it, sweetheart. Blackmail is built. You don't slip into it like a puddle."

"No, yet . . . I don't pretend I'm an angel. But I haven't seen. Try to think of me—well, as a bill collector. I don't start anything; I don't end anything. I begin when the people are already in debt. Oh, I know what you're thinking but try to see that from the middle, where I've been standing, both beginning and end are out of sight. Especially if you don't care to look." Her eyes dropped away from his, hastened back. "Tonight proves that I can never quit. I've always thought of that, put it off, but—don't you see—I can't! I need your help so very desperately. But *how* can you help? They nearly killed me tonight. The next time . . . They had every minute to try. I can't watch every minute!"

"Over the phone, you said *he*."

She ducked, physically, and her voice was muffled against his tie. "Did I? I was nearly frightened senseless. I meant *they*."

"Positive?"

"They, two of them. Men I'd never seen before. One a little fellow with white hair, towheaded. The other was bigger, bulkier, with almost no chin. I answered the door and they forced their way in and locked me in the bedroom. I could hear them—no, not quite hear them—talking about what to do with me. Then, suddenly, I remembered I had carried the telephone into the bedroom to use earlier. It was horrible, Max—my hand could hardly dial. I suppose they heard me. They came . . ." She lifted her face and its wan smile. "The rest of it you know better than I, darling."

"Yes."

Quincy's tropical eyes drifted shut and her mouth swelled tenderly, ready to pay. Amused, Thursday sighed over her face. The moment carried him into the past, into Wednesday, when Yvonne Odler had been making him at home in *her* apartment. Same moment, same lies, his same reaction.

Thursday stood up and Quincy tumbled down his legs to sprawl on her Persian rug. He said, "You turned on a little gas to smell up this place. When you heard me open your door you stuck your pretty head in the oven and turned on some more. No hired killers would debate over what to do with you or leave you alone with a phone or set you up for such an easy rescue after you'd tipped me off. And quit fingering that bruise—I saw you get that this evening when Irene knocked you back on this sofa arm right here." He put on his hat.

"No, no!" Quincy grabbed his legs and began to cry, rubbing her forehead against his knees. "Max, I lied, I lied. Forgive me or don't forgive me, but listen to my reason."

"Why so much trouble to tie my hands?" Thursday asked. "A bullet would shut me up, that's the simple way. Or are you scared of my record—scared I might throw a few back? You might be right so don't try it. No, what I really think is that you don't care much for murder as long as you can scheme up something trickier. How long before you run out of schemes?"

She flung back her head and looked up at him. "Max—how can you say those things to me? How, after today?"

"You mean yesterday. This is another day, Saturday." He flushed at his own stupid, evasive argument. She waited, knowing. He stared down at her eyes which glistened pitifully as did all the rhinestone eyes of the monkey heads across her jacket. He growled, "You kept me entertained all day so I couldn't interfere with something else. What? Was it while somebody moved your blackmail goods from Night & Day to a better hiding place?"

"I can't deny any evil you want to think, Max. But there was more. We told each other then, we both knew it then. Why don't you answer me? Don't use the word love if you're afraid of it, darling. But you know we had more than our subterfuges. I did and you—"

"Okay," he snapped. "Don't maul it around."

"You're ashamed."

Thursday said, more gently, "No. Confused, maybe, because I didn't ask for you to be the way you were—are—but I'm not so confused I can be stopped. You haven't changed the sides any or redrawn the lines. They're still there. No, I'm not sorry I stepped across but I am sorry you can't be rescued from where you stand. But I can't do that."

"I see." Quincy rose to her feet, facing him while she dried her eyes with her forefingers. "All right. I can't do anything but throw myself on your mercy and hope that you do—well, feel something toward me."

Still gently, he said, "What's the truth, if any?"

"No attack, of course. I staged it but not to tie your hands in any way, Max. You're right about my scheming and my trickery. How do you think I've lived my life? I need your help and I had hoped to gain your sympathy."

"And you're hoping now, aren't you?"

"Yes," she admitted. "I have everything to gain, feeling as I do about you. I know your position is exactly opposite—for I do think you feel something, too. Don't answer. I meant what I said before about quitting. And what I pretended had happened tonight *will* happen—unless you can stop it, and I'm not terribly certain about that. I know him too well. He'll never let me leave him."

"Him?"

She whispered, "Rupert," and Thursday grunted. His dropping glance saw her clenched fists against her hips.

"You don't believe me, do you?" Quincy smiled tightly. "You don't believe that I can be this frightened of him. Simply because he doesn't look—"

"No, he doesn't."

She backed away one step. "Very well. Please forget I said anything." Her breathing was suddenly audible. "You'll remember that, won't you—please, darling? *I didn't say anything!*"

"Don't worry," Thursday said absently, squinting. "Where does Rupert hang out when he's not here?"

First, she shook her head violently. Then she caught her breath. "He has insomnia. He roams the streets at night. Sometimes he drinks in an after-hours place at the back of the Liberty Hotel. I don't know if he'd—"

"I'll look." Thursday went to the door. She didn't follow. The view of her apartment that stayed with him was Quincy's oblique eyes, larger than he'd ever seen them, staring after him.

Chapter 26

SATURDAY, AUGUST 13, 2:00 A.M.

The woman was a blowsy fifty, gaunt, and she wore a kimono she had bought in the days when Japanese kimonos were bought. She blocked the open crack of the hotel's back door. "Kitchen's all closed up, my boy. What'd you think?"

"I think you got me wrong."

Her eyes still said cop. Thursday flashed his wallet, the card that confirmed his private license. She flipped through the rest of the wallet, finding nothing that disagreed. "No trouble?"

"No trouble, mother. Just a drink."

"Got to be careful." She closed the door to unchain it, then let him in. He followed her through a storeroom of crates and wilted vegetables, feeling just fine about his occupation. He might look honest, but proving he was a private detective showed the world he wasn't.

The dozen men and women in the big hotel kitchen glanced at him curiously as he entered. They seemed smaller than they should, dominated by the black stoves and cumbersome serving tables and high greasy ceilings. The suspended light bulbs beamed down cruelly, making their ordinariness ugly.

They sat uncomfortably in low-voiced couples or groups on wooden folding chairs. Each held a water tumbler of liquor and there were three open bottles on a butcher block near a faucet. Bourbon, scotch, or rye, with or without water.

The kimono brushed Thursday's elbow like a grimy butterfly. "That'll relieve you of one buck, my boy."

He paid and took his tumbler and strolled over to Rupert, gathering a chair en route. The fat little man sat by himself in a corner behind one of the cold grim stoves. Thursday unfolded his chair and seated himself close to Rupert's right arm.

Rupert looked up, no surprise in his mild smile, and went back to studying the linoleum pattern.

Thursday set his drink on the floor out of the way. "Joint like this is a godsend for an insomniac, isn't it?"

"Yes," Rupert agreed. "Nights can stretch pretty long. Are you troubled by sleeplessness, too, Mr. Thursday?"

"I'm troubled finding time to sleep."

"In that case, I don't understand why you bother with this." Rupert's round belly bounced with a one-syllable chuckle in advance of his making a little joke. "Then again, if you were seeking the most agonizing chairs in the world, you came—"

"I was looking for you." His left arm pressed more firmly against Rupert's pudgy right one but the man made no movement. "Quincy told me where to find you and suggested a couple things I should do when I did find you. But I wanted to chat first, Rupert. Do you have a first name, by the way? Not that it matters—what's half an alias between friends?"

"As you say, it doesn't matter. Excuse me." His right arm stirred suddenly as he transferred his drink to his left hand and then drained the glass. "I don't imagine it matters to anyone."

"It started as a shakedown case but it picked up a pair of murders on its way, like a snowball. You know what happens to snowballs when they get this hot. Something that matters now is who is going to take the rap. In this state, they don't melt that person; they gas him—or her."

"I agree with you, Mr. Thursday. That does matter."

"Nice that our views coincide somewhat. Now do we agree that I hunted you up as a friendly act?"

"If so, I wouldn't understand."

"We both know what Night & Day is, Rupert, and that you belong. But Quincy is measuring you for the entire rap. That's my friendly warning. You're getting built up as the mastermind."

Rupert pursed his lips moistly and silently inspected his empty glass. He cleared his throat softly. "Thank you."

"I wouldn't let her drop you again, sucker. She's all ready to; she's been ready since Showalter made the headlines. She's giving you the identical treatment she gave you in Cleveland in '42. Dr. Newman. That time you went to prison to protect Hilda Graves. Protecting Quincy Day will take a lot more out of you."

Rupert said again, "Thank you."

"You're a big boy now, doctor, too big to be a football no matter how pretty the foot. I nearly split a gut when Quincy announced you were the brains of her outfit. You're not smart enough and you're not man enough." The taunting didn't take. The fat man blinked occasionally but no spark lit his meek colorless eyes.

"Why do you stand for it?" Thursday asked. "You don't think she loves you, do you?"

Rupert said, as if to soothe him, "Now really, Mr. Thursday,

I don't believe I care to discuss it, if it's all the same to you."

"You were there tonight, according to the elevator boy, just before she got the great idea of phoning me up. You don't have insomnia, Rupert—you just don't have any place to sleep half the time."

"Please, Mr. Thursday—"

"It gets difficult to feel sorry for you, so why should I waste my time on it? Go ahead. Take the fall for that tramp. She's got you tabbed right."

Rupert's bulk stiffened. His neutral voice was imperative for the first time. "Don't call her that."

"Nicest word I could think of. I wouldn't want this mixed company to overhear me calling that slut a—"

Rupert shifted suddenly, his right hand diving into his coat pocket. Thursday's hand streaked after it, down to the cool hidden metal of the automatic. His finger got inside the trigger guard, behind the trigger so it couldn't be pulled. He could feel a roll of bloated waist against his hand and the soft finger in front of the trigger which Rupert wouldn't remove. The two men sat stiffly side by side, both with a hand buried in the coat pocket.

Thursday breathed, "Let go," and Rupert's face only jelled into stubborn folds. "Okay, then." Thursday commenced bending the unseen gun upward, stripping Rupert's trigger finger back toward its chubby wrist. There was a soft pop of sound.

Rupert bit his lip, and his face sagged in defeat. Thursday withdrew both their hands, without the gun. The swift vicious conflict had attracted no attention. On the other side of the stove, a middle-aged man and a young girl bubbled the same conversation as before.

Thursday said softly, "That'll keep you from doing anything you ought to think twice about."

Rupert stared at him a moment, as if there might be something in the detective's face he wanted to know. Then he looked down again, at his broad thighs where lay the hand with the broken forefinger. He looked at it as he looked at everything, submissively.

As Thursday rose, he picked up his tumbler of whisky and fitted it into Rupert's good hand and got another "Thank you."

The slattern in the kimono called out, "Come back again, my boy," as Thursday crossed the kitchen. At the doorway, he looked back at Rupert. The whisky was finished already and from the hopeless way Rupert's head drooped forward Thursday guessed he was crying.

Chapter 27

SATURDAY, AUGUST 13, 3:00 A.M.

Thursday was hanging his coat in his closet when the knock came. He let Vespasian in. The little man slipped past him and glanced quickly into the other rooms. Then he said, "Just protecting myself," and took off the cheap tan cloth hat he had bought and scratched around his tape. "I was waiting across the street until you got home, Maxie. Didn't want to beat up your front door any more."

"I saw you being inconspicuous behind the bush."

"You might have given me the high sign."

"And spoil your fun?" Thursday held out his hand. "Produce."

Vespasian tossed him the keys Coffee had made. "One opens up the building, one opens all office doors to this Night & Day outfit, and one opens a special little file in one of the private offices."

"Which office?"

"The one marked Mr. Rupert."

"What happened to the night watchman in the downstairs lobby, by the way?"

Vespasian smirked. "He was called away by the noise of a breaking window. Nothing to it, Maxie."

"The list."

"The money."

Thursday gave him two more tens. In exchange he got a long torn strip of buff-colored paper. The column of names was pencil-written in a flamboyant hand.

From his wallet, Thursday unfolded the brown envelope flap on which he had copied the names involved in Don Kerner's cache. He sat down by the office table and began comparing. On the back of his neck he could almost feel Vespasian's puzzled frown. The checking of names took five minutes, and the two rosters matched except for order. The Vespasian list was shorter by one name than the Kerner list: Perry Showalter.

"Well, Maxie, I guess I better get on my horse." Vespasian shuffled nervously and Thursday grinned up at him.

"Worried? You're in good standing for a change."

"Yeah, but how come you had those same names already? What was I doing risking my tail if you already had them? Maxie, you wouldn't be setting me up for something?"

"No, of course not," Thursday said softly. He crumpled the original list—the one in his own handwriting—and set fire to it in an ashtray.

"I just wouldn't try it, brother. I got a big mouth on occasion."

"Don't fret. And don't rush off." Thursday fingered the shiny side of the heavy paper Vespasian had used, absently read the watermark: TITE. The paper folded bulkily, taking up a lot of room in his wallet. "Why didn't you write on a piece of linoleum and be done with it?"

"I didn't know you wanted it on high-class A-1 monogrammed stationery. I just picked up the first piece of paper I found lying around the office. Any more questions?"

"Let's see." Smiling, Thursday rose and patted over Vespasian's pockets. The little man sighed submissively. From his shirt pocket, over the cast, Thursday drew a sheaf of bills. He counted them. "Two hundred and forty-four dollars. Where from?"

Vespasian winked. "It happened to be lying around in the old cashbox, my friend. You wanted this deal to look like a burglary, didn't you?"

Thursday peeled off thirty dollars and stuck the rest back in the shirt pocket. "You don't need my chicken feed. Okay, on your way. Suppose you hole up in the Old Spanish Auto Camp, on Pacific by Cudahy Slough."

"Sure," Vespasian said. "Call me there."

Thursday smiled. "I wouldn't waste my nickel. You're about to drop out of sight on your own. I don't think you trust me, Vespasian."

"Why, whatever gave you that idea, Maxie? I love anybody that puts me in the way of two hundred and fourteen free bucks. I'll be there."

"You keep lying. You're not out of bait yet."

Vespasian unwrapped a stick of chewing gum thoughtfully. "You're almost right, Maxie. I got one gimmick. I got a reason somebody wants me dead. But until I can remember what I got I don't know how to spring it. So I'm going to hide and think until it comes to me."

"Then you'll go out and let them finish blowing you apart."

"Maybe." He popped the gum into his mouth and began chewing while he grinned contemplatively at Thursday on the divan. "And maybe I'll apply the old gray matter this trip. Maybe I'll let you spring the gimmick for me—if we can arrange terms. I'll call you." Vespasian opened the front door.

Thursday said, "You been pretending not to know who Fathom's friends are. Yet I discussed that point with the late Colonel right under your itchy nose. The somebody who wants you stuffed and mounted is Quincy Day, his boss."

Vespasian jiggled the door lightly by its knob. "I thought you'd passed that over. Well, here's the straight dope. My angle—"

"You'll find she's a charming lady with a gang and hardly any blood on her hands at all. She lives in the Frémont Hotel. You go ahead—run over and tell her you put the finger on Fathom and robbed her office. Make a deal. I got a hunch I'll make great strides once you're a body and not fiddling up the facts any more. Good night."

"No!" Vespasian burst out. "You got all the wrong slant, Maxie. I'm just taking care of myself, watching out for number one. Look, I'm going to cut you in once I think of what I got to think of." His lips worked up a fleeting confident smile that looked ready to snap under the pressure of some vague fear. "You wait."

Thursday yawned. "Good night."

"I'll call you sure. Well . . ." Vespasian pulled his cheap hat lower, glanced outside, hesitated as if he wanted to say something more and then vanished around the edge of the door.

Thursday got up and bolted the screen and locked the door and turned off the living room lights. In the bedroom he looked at his alarm clock. Three-thirty. He grimaced and set it for eight and got ready for bed.

A long time later he was still awake, staring at the indefinite reaches of the ceiling. It was too warm to sleep under anything more than a sheet and that weighed on his lanky, tense body heavily. He tried to like himself, what he was doing, and couldn't. He wanted a cigarette but couldn't bring himself to get up and it touched his mind obliquely that smoking in bed was against the law. At that he laughed out loud, harshly. The sound hushed itself in the dark.

The day the Whitney case had commenced lapping around his ankles, he had made Irene quite a noble speech about ethics. Since then he had tampered with evidence and lied to the authorities. He had even hidden Don Kerner from the law, although the law didn't know it wanted him yet.

No, Thursday reflected, he hadn't exactly trod a moral path this week. He tried to remember where he had turned off the main road. He had taken Irene's case because he had respected her and wanted to protect her from an insidious business. Thursday snorted; at the time, he had also wanted to spread his reputation around among her rich friends. "No use playing Galahad at this time of night," he muttered to himself. The facts were: once in the case, he had gotten mad at the extortionists and intended to break them one way or another.

He couldn't convince himself he had played completely fair even with his client. For Quincy was the enemy, and his interlude with Quincy hadn't been strictly in the line of duty. Confusing, when he liked both Irene and Quincy as abstract persons...

Yet—he had advanced his client's interests somewhat by using Quincy. He sighed and tried to make up his mind whether he really needed that cigarette or not. But all he could concentrate on were the most intangible aspects of means and end. He was still convinced that the end he had in view was right and proper. On the other hand, his methods thus far weren't. They would never be, even with that right and proper end achieved. But—did justification matter? Clapp would think so, but Clapp, admittedly wiser, was also in an official position where a certain amount of principle was forced upon him. Clapp didn't think that any moral result could be obtained through immorality.

"Neither does Thursday—in theory," Thursday comforted himself. Clapp said that this tricky stuff always ended up as a taste in your mouth. Thursday told himself that at least he wasn't being unbendingly righteous, there was that. He yawned with disgust at his misplaced whimsicality, thought he was ready to sleep, found a comfortable position, and was immediately more wide awake than ever.

Protect Irene. And, incidentally, protect her husband. That was irony with bells on. *Find Nell Kopke.* Find why she had gone through the motions of leaving town. That was the obvious next step. But would the discovery of Nell Kopke have any bearing on the really vital problem? The vital problem was to find the *key*.

Murder was murder but Thursday also had the client's interests to look after first. So—the key was most important. Somewhere within reach was a theoretical strongbox where Quincy had locked her store of blackmail evidence including the Irene Whitney IOUs.

Thursday pondered drowsily. Quincy undoubtedly kept the stuff in a Night & Day safe during calm periods. She would have moved it to a hideaway when the trouble started. Where?

He doubted that the mythical key was one of those copied by Coffee. No, Quincy wouldn't leave such a key lying around her apartment. And the key didn't necessarily have to be a metal one with wards and webs; it might well be a cardboard claim check or a few words over the telephone.

Find the key.

Under misty visions of a thousand kinds of keys, Thursday fell asleep, and when the keys began to jangle that was the alarm clock saying eight o'clock. He had gotten an hour's sleep.

He padded groggily out to the kitchen in his pajamas, drank a glass of water, lit a cigarette, and sat down over the telephone.

First and needlessly, to give his head time to clear, he dialed Yvonne Odler's apartment at The Devonshire. After a long ringing, she said, "Hello" sleepily and he hung up. It gave him a small mean pleasure and it confirmed what he had been sure of, anyway; people named Odler didn't go to jail.

To his next call, Merle Osborn answered just as sleepily. He bantered gently for a few minutes before getting to the point. "There's a favor you can do me, honey. I think there'll be a minor burglary report on the blotter today. Night & Day for some two hundred bucks. Suppose you play it for ten times more than it's worth. Detailed interviews with everyone connected with the organization and lots of pictures of the staff and office interiors and so on. Then give the thing all the nice black *Sentinel* publicity the traffic will bear."

"Well—it *can* be done. But an awfully good question occurs to me, darling. Why?"

"I'm up to something."

"Why, you smug devil you!" Merle drawled. "Always the operator."

He grunted, irritated by the truth. She had jabbed with the same needle he had used on himself all last night. "It's for a good cause," Thursday said dryly. "No holds barred in some fights, you know. I'm trying to scare somebody and any opening I can throw something at. I'm going to do it."

"Well, for heaven's sakes, don't get mad, Thursday! I'll do it for you but you better go back to bed and get up right."

He calmed down, they talked some more and after she had said goodbye, he called the local office of the State Board of Equalization and asked the secretary for Samuel Ulrich, please.

"Sam, there's a favor you can do me."

Ulrich's laugh boomed in the receiver. "I haven't got one thing else to do, you know that, Thursday."

"Don't worry, you won't have to turn a hand. I want some legwork from your dry spies while they're out making sure the liquor customers are over kindergarten age. Or maybe one of your boys will recognize the bar I have in mind."

"If it's a bar in the country, one of the bunch will have been in it. What's the details?"

Thursday paused, marshaling his facts. He was certain it was a bar Nell Kopke had phoned from last night because she had been drinking then, as she had since Papago's death. He said, "Well, it's some place in the fifteen-cent phone toll district. That narrows it down to Del Mar, Jamacha, San Ysidro, Jamul, or some highway joint near there. There's a pay phone but I don't think it's in a booth. Right next to the phone there's a pin ball machine—one of those that buzzes everytime your marble bounces off a post. And there's a jukebox but it isn't very near the phone. Oh, and the jukebox still has Freddie Martin's 'Polonaise' on it."

Ulrich said, "Whew," and laughed again, uproariously.

"Can you ask around, Sam? It's pretty important. I'll fork over ten bucks to whatever dry spy gives me a lead—double that if the lead pays off."

"Boy, they'll jump at the deal, being on government wages. Me, you owe a drink to, Thursday. I'll ask around. Since it's Saturday, the bunch'll be in and out. This is our busy day. I'll call you."

"No. I'll call you from time to time, Sam. Thanks a million."

He put the phone away and deliberated what he wanted to do next. Taking a hint from the quality of his thinking, he went back to bed for a little more sleep.

The doorbell woke him at four-thirty.

Thursday opened the door and faced three men. One he didn't know, one was a burly man from the D.A.'s office named Barnes, and the third, the leader, was Ed Wales. Wales gave his shallow young grin and said, "You certainly do sleep late, Max. You must have a secret of success." He looked self-satisfied.

"Come on in," Thursday growled and unbolted the screen. "What's Benedict's beef now?"

The trio filed in. Wales said, more seriously, "You know he's a square shooter, Max. He admits he dislikes you personally so he's leaning over backward to be fair."

"Get to the point."

Wales frowned pompously. "Mr. Benedict thought you'd agree to a private chat in his office before you were booked."

Thursday stared. "Booked! On what charge?"

"Suspicion of murder of Ellis Fathom."

CHAPTER 28

SATURDAY, AUGUST 13, 5:00 P.M.

The district attorney's office was as shabby as most in the eighty-year-old county courthouse. A corner room on the first floor, its high narrow windows pierced one drab plaster wall for a view of Front Street and the side of the Pickwick Hotel, and pierced another to show the courthouse lawn where sailors loafed and watched Broadway's passing sideshow. It was a shabby office, and only Leslie Benedict's cool presence behind his desk invested the place with lofty aims.

Thursday sat in front of the dark old desk, lighting a cigarette and hoping the dampness he felt on his forehead would be attributed to the waning heat of the day. He told himself he wasn't exactly worried; but he was worried that he ought to be worried. Behind him, he could sense every breath of big young Wales who stood sentry by the locked door. On the other side of the door stood a uniformed patrolman. Barnes and the other D.A. man had returned to Thursday's house to exercise their search warrant, having delivered him here.

Pulling a spotless ashstand nearer, Thursday smiled across the desk. "Well, any time."

Benedict's short mouth said, "I presume Mr. Wales explained to you the reason for my procedure in dealing with you. If you feel you'd rather summon your lawyer, we can proceed with formal arrest and booking."

"No. I'll play."

"Very well. I want to give you every chance to answer the allegations beforehand because I am personally prejudiced against you, Thursday. I'm convinced that you killed Ellis Fathom. However, Lieutenant Clapp, with whom I consulted because of your close relationship, maintains the possibility that you are merely withholding valuable information. I say *merely* in a comparative sense."

"Okay. You want to horse-trade."

His yellow eyes flickered and Benedict said, "Not at all. I want the truth."

Thursday sucked stolidly on his cigarette, wondering how much more weight he could carry alone. Barnes and the other man would find nothing in his house. But he had two items in his pockets that would come to light when he was booked. The copied set of Quincy's keys probably wouldn't mean anything to anybody. But in his wallet was the list of Quincy's extortion victims. He hadn't had a chance to get rid of it. Of course, it was in Vespasian's handwriting but it might be very damaging.

Thursday could feel the two men watching him think. He shrugged casually to prove he wasn't bothered and tried to weed out his facts. How much was excess baggage? What could he shed without endangering . . . Irene gazed back at him from a new silver frame on her husband's desk. The photograph was evidently new, too, since she was wearing her hair as she had last Monday. He hauled in his wandering mind and tried to consider the *now*.

"Well?" Benedict asked curtly.

"Oh, you waiting for me? I thought you were going to explain how I killed Fathom so I could start knocking over your ducks."

Benedict folded his hands—the polished, perfect nails irritated Thursday—and led off. "The finest cases sometimes are woven from hundreds of details. In this instance, we not only have this web of matching minutiae but it is sustained by certain dominant strands, solid bases which I doubt you can explain away. A very principal basis, Thursday, is your own record. You're a known killer. You've killed four people and gotten away with it."

"The coroner gave me a clean bill of health," Thursday said wearily.

"Certainly. Self-defense. Justifiable homicide, although I detest the term. The victims were criminals. But the fact remains that you have had no compunction about taking human life in the past. And there we have an extremely vital strand on which to build the rest: predisposition."

"You're making me feel better, Benedict. Before you started talking I thought you might have something."

"I have. Let's first examine the murder of George Papago. Here is where the constant sifting of police reports begins to develop the whole. On the night Papago was bludgeoned to death, Officer Gannette found you prowling around a car which was parked two blocks from the bar where the victim was last seen alive. The car has since been identified as belonging to the victim."

"Maybe you're talking about a man answering my description and one of a thousand Chrysler convertibles."

"A man of your description—very well. Detail number two: this man of your description followed Papago for several hours that evening, expressing every intent of overtaking him. According to eyewitnesses at the bar in question—McCloskey's Shining Hour—you did overtake him and induced him to leave the bar with you. I've arranged that you meet those witnesses in the regular lineup this evening."

Thursday chuckled. "All I'm getting out of your opening address are signs of overconfidence and a lot of confusion. Aren't you going to tag me with the Fathom killing?"

"I'll come to that. Detail number three: the day Papago's body was discovered, you brought the victim's bloodstained hat to Lieutenant Clapp with a trumped-up story. This maneuver obviously sprang from your congenital braggartry and desire for newspaper publicity."

"Except that I didn't bring any hat to Clapp. I uncovered a legitimate suspect and forced him to turn in that evidence."

"Suspect? Undoubtedly—but accomplice is a more inclusive word. Especially since this Vespasian disappeared from

County Hospital under rather mysterious circumstances. We're quite anxious to hear *his* story of the Fathom ambush."

Wales put in, "If and when we find him alive."

"So I doubt if you're counting on much support from this Vespasian, Thursday. I'd be willing to guarantee that you've put him out of the way by now, which would make your third attempt on his life."

Thursday laughed. "Time was when your badgering might have riled me, Benedict. Not any more. Any time I need a laugh, I'll think back to this session and thank you."

Benedict's smooth face didn't change. He proceeded as if he were dictating a letter. "So stands the Papago case with those three salient and damning details. You'll grant there are links between Papago and Fathom, three links. Yourself, the Papago-Fathom meeting at the McCloskey bar Monday night, and Vespasian's unexplained connection with both affairs."

"I'll grant the last two."

"Now, let's examine detail number four. This morning Mr. Wales, with a proper warrant and accompanied by other of my investigators, entered your office in the Moulton Building. We took this action upon complaint by a daughter of one of our leading citizens."

"That would be Yvonne Odler."

Wales grunted I-told-you-so. Benedict looked at Thursday reproachfully as if he shouldn't have spoken the name so flippantly. Thursday stared back while he stomped out his cigarette in the ashstand and lit another. He asked over his shoulder, "What did you find, champ?"

Benedict answered for his assistant, icily. "The point here is not what my investigators found but the nature of Miss Odler's complaint. For some time you have been blackmailing her by means of lascivious photographs for which she was induced to pose."

"Photographs you didn't find don't make much of a case, do they?" Thursday blew a smoke ring across the desk. "You know this reminds me of a double-action frame that happened to an acquaintance of mine in San Berdoo. He was a private cop, too, and he was getting in people's hair. The second half of the rig is all that applies here. These hairy people had a phony client leave some hot material in his office for safe-keeping, and then the so-called client showed up with the cops later. But he had caught on and burned the pictures fast—and since he hadn't taken a retainer or signed any receipts he was in the clear. Lucky for him, too."

Again Benedict's expression didn't alter and Thursday began to wonder what big thing he was reserving to win this duel. Behind his back, Wales murmured, "Frame. Now where have I heard that before?"

Thursday snapped, without turning around. "Probably in court, every time you cross-examine a private cop. Some ex-cons get licensed here and there so that makes crowbait of all of us."

"Persecution complex," Wales said.

Thursday snorted. "Let's compare a couple examples. Me and Yvonne Odler. Through a leak you would deplore, Benedict, I've learned that last Wednesday the untouchable Odler was picked up on a morals charge that was backed by plenty of evidence. But she's sobered up and let loose, probably with an apology. Today I'm arrested and my layout is searched on that tramp's say-so. I'll go out of here cleared but with another crack in my reputation. Since reputations are pretty fragile in my business, I make a good defenseless target."

"No such leak exists," said Benedict calmly. "You gained that information firsthand. You see, the remainder of Miss Odler's allegation declared that when she was no longer able to pay you extortion, you entrapped her in her apartment last Wednesday afternoon. You were attempting to tarnish *her* reputation, as revenge or as an example, I suppose. You were assisted by an accomplice. Abe Shahan. Shahan has confessed, Thursday. He admits to being your assistant, to taking the photographs you destroyed, and to aiding in said entrapment. Shahan is still under detention, of course."

"And I still say frame, Benedict. Shahan's being used to run me off the road, which ought to prove I'm on the right road and dangerous. Shahan gets a big payoff and the parole system will cushion his fall. Meanwhile, my word as a legitimate businessman is canceled by that of Shahan—who is a known criminal." The last was an easy guess.

"He is," admitted Benedict, "but his story is corroborated by Miss Odler's statement. She isn't—not on your say-so."

"Naturally, Miss Odler will be completely protected by your office. Mystery Witness Points Accusing Finger, et cetera."

"You would know the jargon." Benedict smiled briefly. "Now we see the motive taking definite shape. It has long been my suspicion that a well organized extortion ring was operating here in San Diego. The Perry Showalter suicide provided the first concrete lead, and we are tracing others. For example, I have here a report concerning an incident at the firm Night & Day, where you obviously terrorized the owner, Miss Day. I don't doubt that she'll develop into another valuable witness against you, and there'll appear many more now that the ball is rolling."

"Isn't that your first compliment, Benedict? So I'm the brains."

"You may consider it brains, I suppose. Yes, this office believes you to be the man behind this outbreak of extortion. It's a pattern which occurs not infrequently among men of your so-called legitimate profession. You murdered Papago because he was interfering. You murdered Fathom—who was once Showalter's valet—because he knew too much."

Thursday grunted unbelievingly and shook his head, mimicking a daze. "I've never seen conjecture piled this high before. I think you're sick, Benedict. You've got obsessions."

"Indeed? You've been anxious to narrow this discussion down to the actual circumstances of the Fathom murder. Very well. Detail number five: Ellis Fathom was shot to death with a .32 caliber revolver. On Wednesday morning in your office, according to the report of Officer Hoover, you claimed possession of a .32 caliber Colt revolver. This despite your repeated statements in the past to this office and to police headquarters that you neither own nor carry a gun. Which you are not licensed to do, incidentally."

"I turned that license back in, of my own free will, nearly a year ago. Don't twist it."

"That's by the way. You did have this revolver and you did admit ownership. That's a matter of record."

"Keep it coming."

"Detail number six: a man of your description was seen hurrying away one block west of the Fathom shooting which occurred within easy walking distance of your home. According to Lieutenant Clapp, you have no worth-while alibi for the time in question. Correct me if I'm wrong." Conclusively, Benedict unlaced his fingers and leaned forward on his desk, face grim. "Detail number seven: during Mr. Wales' investigation of your office this morning, he discovered a bullet imbedded in your wall. He extracted that bullet which, being stopped only by a map mounted on beaverboard and old plaster behind that, showed clear striations for identification purposes. It came, you told Officer Hoover, from the .32 revolver you claimed as your own. The ballistics report proves conclusively that the bullet was fired from the same revolver you used to kill Ellis Fathom!"

CHAPTER 29

SATURDAY, AUGUST 13, 5:30 P.M.

The room was stifling and the walls at that moment seemed to move in on him. Thursday could feel his facial muscles stiffening grotesquely. Benedict now leaned back in his chair and observed. He had made his point and was quietly pleased with the result but he did not gloat because he was all business. Thursday wanted to go over to the Front Street windows which were half-raised and drink in some air. But he also didn't want to give himself away any more. Somehow, he smiled woodenly, saying, "For a moment there you threw a real scare into me. Don't think I haven't got answers, though."

Then he realized he was talking right through Wales's comments. ". . . puzzles me, Max, is why you didn't extract the bullet yourself and, say, substitute an unincriminating slug. Of course, such action would have ruined your wall map as I had to do. I imagine you thought the original hole would go without notice since it was pretty small. I only discovered it myself by merest chance."

"I didn't think it was important," Thursday said. "Shouldn't that prove something?"

Benedict shook his long head no.

Thursday again glanced involuntarily at the cool unscreened windows but took a deep breath where he was. He *didn't* have answers; there was no answer to circumstances. Quincy's attempts to tie him up were kid games compared to what he had accidentally done to himself. He lit another cigarette, stalling, knowing Benedict knew it. He said, "Well, the .32 in question belonged to Nell Kopke," and told the story of Wednesday's incident swiftly.

Benedict rationed out another small smile. "That hardly fits the facts. You simply happen to know that the Kopke woman owned a .32 caliber Colt revolver. We were already aware of that since the gun is registered. But you haven't taken into consideration that both woman and child left San Diego before the Fathom shooting."

"Yes, she shipped her furniture east and left on the streamliner with a long ticket. But she didn't have to change to the eastbound in L.A. She could have changed to anything that brought her back south and she had the time. What if I told you Nell Kopke was back in town?"

"I would say you were attempting to gain time."

Thursday grunted, selected another card. "Joaquin Vespasian can prove I didn't shoot Fathom."

"Indeed? And where is Vespasian? Do you know?"

"No. But I'm the only guy in town he might let find him. Suppose you give me twenty-four hours to bring him in. In fact, twenty-four hours will let me wrap this whole case up for you."

"You're bargaining." Benedict's skin darkened angrily. "I don't care for bargaining, Thursday, as you know. I want truth, verifiable truth."

Thursday shrugged. He didn't go much himself for the idea of counting on Vespasian as a witness. While he thought over the remainder of his hand, he said, "And when I'm on ice, the really criminal element will keep giving you the runaround. I'm getting tired of the drip-drip-drip of your personal dislike for me, Benedict. You're too honest to frame me but you're taking every advantage of some silly coincidences."

"I am well aware," said Benedict stonily, "of the contempt you hold for my office and the law in general. As for any personal—"

"I've worked pretty well with some legal branches in the past. Isn't that entered in my file? Or isn't there a credit column?"

"You may have worked with the police when it furthered your own devices. As for any personal animosity, I am giving you every opportunity to explain your appearance of guilt. If you haven't any explanations grounded in fact—well . . ."

"Okay." Thursday grimaced morosely. "I'm throwing my insurance policy into the pot and I hope you have sense enough to use it right. Two days ago I had a guy tucked away in the Coronado jail for safekeeping. He's a local photo studio man named Don Kerner and I had him booked under the name James Donald. Get him over here and listen to him name a few real names in this blackmail mess. He's all yours and you can claim you uncovered him yourself. I promise I won't tell the papers different."

Benedict sat still, his cold gaze playing over Thursday. After a moment, he murmured, "Very well, we'll see," and lifted the nearest telephone receiver.

Thursday looked around at Ed Wales who smiled pleasantly and emptily. Thursday lifted a corner of his own mouth and turned his back on him again. He stared into the eyes of Irene's photograph, wondering. Outside his mind, he heard Benedict's indistinguishable droning into the phone. He wondered whether Kerner's testimony would be enough to get him twenty-four hours' freedom. With a couple breaks, he might be able to trick Quincy out of the IOUs—with a couple breaks and a little time to set up something . . .

Benedict hung up and Thursday raised his head. The district attorney said, "The prisoner booked as James Donald is no longer in the Coronado jail. Bail was posted for him this morning by a man named Rupert. So this so-called witness—Kerner, you called him?—was set free."

"Huh?" Thursday felt the slow sinking in his stomach. The walls moved in on him again and the air was hot and thick, not enough to breathe. "They found him after all," he said to no one in particular.

And no one in particular was listening. The other two were gazing through him, Benedict dispassionately, and Wales as a reflection. Benedict said, "So suppose we cease talking about nonexistent testimony and discuss the possibility of your making a formal statement."

Wales added, "Or do you have another ace up your sleeve, Max?"

Thursday said, "Let me think a minute." He tore his eyes away from the picture of Irene Benedict and got heavily to his feet. He moved toward the windows to get some air into his constricted throat.

Wales said warningly, "Now, I wouldn't attempt anything foolish."

Afterwards, Thursday told himself he wouldn't have thought of it alone. Afterwards, he told himself he wouldn't have acted on Wales's suggestion if the big young man hadn't strolled across the office after him and laid a restraining hand on his shoulder.

But the physical touch of the closing trap was too much. He lost his temper. Growling, he spun around and smashed a fist into Wales's smile. Wales reeled backward against Benedict's chair and they both fell to the floor.

Deep in Thursday's brain there was no reactive picture of what he had done. The single impulse, there and throughout his body, was to be free of the narrowing walls. He thrust the window higher, vaulted, and felt the sting on his feet as they splatted on the courthouse sidewalk outside.

He began to run, sprinting across Front Street into the Greyhound Bus tunnel behind the Pickwick Hotel. In the cavern, he slowed to a speedy walk and came out on the other side of the block.

Four minutes later he was at the Plaza, boarding a La Mesa bus.

CHAPTER 30

SATURDAY, AUGUST 13, 7:00 P.M.

Quickly, Irene Benedict let him enter her cold, classic house. "I heard," she said. "I halfway expected you."

"I'd like to hear, too," Thursday said. "Where's the short wave?" He sensed the blonde woman's unwillingness as she turned and led him toward her husband's study. Reproach even rustled in the skirt of her black frock.

Her voice floated back over her shoulder, flatly. "You told him? About me?"

"No." In the prim study, he pulled a chair up before the massive console radio and began searching for KMA 363 on the short-wave band. "I needed a safe base of operations and this seemed to be it. Your husband will be busy for a few hours—" he chuckled mirthlessly "—and this is the last place he'd look for me." The radio façade was warm and he asked, "You been using this thing?"

"Certainly. I sometimes do for amusement. That's how I knew about you."

The toneless voice of the police announcer rose and Thursday listened. He found it hard to believe the impersonal announcements were about him. ". . . suspicion of murder. This man may be armed. KMA . . ." He sighed and turned the volume down. The search was still centered in the metropolitan area. They had impounded his Olds. A prowl car had been stationed by the Moulton Building.

Irene's pale-blue eyes were looking down at him—the swelling had gone from the bruised one—and her lips were tight against her teeth. "That's why you're here, isn't it? To use me against my husband." Her words rattled at him like a snake. "It's useless, you know. The threat of scandal would never stop Leslie. Furthermore, I shall deny anything you might tell him. I'll chance that my gambling notes will never be used and deny that I ever hired you. Now I'd prefer that you leave."

"Thanks," Thursday said softly. He rested back in the chair and stared up at her until she looked away. He said, "I happened to escape from your husband's office because I lost my temper. It's the most foolish move I've ever made and unless I can go back with something in my hand, I'm cooked for sure. I thought about you a lot while Benedict was sewing me up. I was wondering whether I could count on you coming forward—voluntarily—to support my word if things got really bad. I see I couldn't. But I would never have used you as a life preserver any other way. I'm an honest man myself though you'd never know it—not at the bottom of this pit I dug trying to save your pretty hide."

Irene turned away. Voice muffled, she asked, "Then what do you want?"

"Just a telephone, sweetheart." She nodded slightly, her back toward him. He got up and went over to sit on the desk. "I asked our district attorney for twenty-four hours to clear this mess up. I was bluffing at the time. Now . . ." He dialed.

The Telephone Secretarial Service had one important call listed. A Mr. Joaquin Vespasian had called his office at six o'clock but had left no number. Thursday had mixed feelings about that, mostly frustrated ones. Vespasian sounded ready to deal again. But there was no way to bait the little man into the open without advertising his own whereabouts, which was impossible because of the police net. Deadlock.

He tried Quincy's apartment and no one answered. He called Merle Osborn, told her to stick by a phone because he might need her, and hung up on her worried pleas to take care of himself. He called Coffee and two other trusted contacts and told them the same thing.

It made him feel better to build this apparatus around the county, to pretend he wasn't alone tonight. Finally, he faced the important call, the one he kept putting off. He dialed Samuel Ulrich's house and talked for a moment with a baby sitter. Then he caught up with Ulrich at a party at the Officers' Club on Harbor Drive.

Thursday's heart skipped a beat when Ulrich's gay, liquored voice said, "One of the bunch knew just the place. I expected you to call all afternoon, thought of nothing else. This roadside tavern fills the bill. Wall pay phone and pinball machine. Jukebox and 'Polonaise' at the other end. My boy's a Martin fan. Maybe you know him. A fellow named—"

"Fine. Where's the place?"

"A mile, maybe two, north of San Ysidro on 101. Tavern called the Lucky Monkey for no discernible reason. Reasonably law-abiding too, I understand."

Thursday said thanks a million and shut him off. He replaced the receiver shakily. A lead toward Nell Kopke meant quite a bit tonight. She might have nothing vital to tell, but proof that she had not gone east would prop up one of those assertions he had made to Benedict. He looked at Irene's trim back. "Want to help?" he asked quietly.

"Certainly, Max." She turned to face him with a shyness that sat awkwardly on an older woman. She got her eyes up to his. "I don't know how to act under a strain. I know my responsibility to you but after a point I can't allow—not to Leslie—do you understand what—"

"Skip it." Thursday grinned, not feeling like it. "Don't analyze. Get a coat, and a scarf to hide your hair. I want you to drive me to San Ysidro. Let's see, if we take that little road through Sunnyside and Bonita, that'll bring us out on 101 without going inside city limits. Odds'll be with us."

The Mexican border was seventeen miles south of San Diego, and San Ysidro was the tiny town a mile north of the border, inland but officially a port. In Irene's blue Buick convertible they rode through a half hour of mysterious citrus groves and moonlit dairy farms before sighting the sky glow of San Ysidro.

"Pull in here," Thursday said. A brighter glow flashed on and off from the sign over a barnlike structure beside the highway. The light bulbs spelled out Lucky Monkey Tavern.

Leaving Irene in the car, he went in to join the Saturday night customers. He bought a beer for show and struck up a leering acquaintance with a satin-slacked waitress. She primped and leaned her blouse over his table and eventually she talked.

Ten minutes later, when he climbed into the convertible beside Irene, he said, "Turn around and go back toward San

Diego—about three-quarters of a mile. A woman and small boy, strangers in town, have rented a place called the Dickey ranch."

Irene obeyed silently. When he said, "There," she turned off the highway onto a rutty lane and they jounced between broad weedy fields that had been plowed some time ago but never planted. She murmured, "No lights in the house."

"This may be nothing except a ride, I don't know," Thursday said hopelessly. He squinted ahead at the rundown cottage on top of a barren knoll. Then he squeezed the woman's arm and she stopped the car a hundred feet short of the house.

In the shallow ditch beside the lane stood a tiny figure, his big eyes gleaming into the headlights like an animal at bay. It was Georgie, his pinched face dirt-streaked and uglier than ever from crying.

Thursday jumped out and strode over to him and the youngster cowered. Thursday said, "Georgie, remember me? I'm a friend of yours."

The youngster whimpered and looked around. Irene brushed by Thursday. "You're frightening him, Max. He's terrified, the poor child, out here alone in the dark." She said soothingly, bending toward him, "Come here, darling. It's all right."

Georgie hesitated, staring around at the ghostly night. Then he flung himself forward into the woman's arms. She stroked his wild black hair and hugged him and whispered, "Poor child." Then, fiercely, "Doesn't anyone take care of him?"

Thursday said, "Find out if he knows where his mother is."

The boy's face was buried in Irene's coat, and he had nothing but dry sobs left. She spoke to him gently.

"She won't say nothing!" Georgie choked. "Mommy won't talk to me!"

Irene said, "Max, we'd better not upset him any more."

"I've got to find her."

"She won't talk to me!" Georgie mumbled against Irene's breast. "Mommy's sick or something!"

Watching the two clasped together in the headlight glow, Thursday felt a chill. The little grimy hand gripping Irene's shoulder had a dab of red color between the fingers.

"Wait here." He got a flashlight out of the glove compartment and stalked up the slope to the little house. The door opened to his touch, and his beam played inside. The pool of light froze after a single sweep.

He knelt beside Nell Kopke's body.

For an unknown time, he was without thought. His hard face bowed over the form on the worn carpet and he felt only that his eyes burned.

When he rose, his teeth bared in a snarl but his throat made no sound. The light moved ahead of him through the shabby house. He found what he was after in a dresser drawer: Nell's .32 Colt revolver.

It was fully loaded with nickel-jacketed bullets, and freshly cleaned. Then, on the wooden bottom of the nearly empty drawer, his probing light beam revealed a droplet of oil. On the pure glistening surface of the minute hemisphere floated something that sparkled. He had to put his eye close to detect that it was an almost microscopic metal filing.

Thursday sucked in his breath and examined the blue-steel gun more closely. Then he dropped it in his coat pocket and left the house.

Irene Benedict was sitting in the car, rocking Georgie gently. His eyes were closed but he gasped convulsively now and then. Irene's cheeks were wet. "She's dead, isn't she?" she whispered.

Thursday nodded and sank onto the seat beside her. "Kid asleep?"

"Yes."

He got out the revolver and turned it over and over in his hands. "She was shot three or four times with her own gun. Probably this afternoon and probably when the kid was playing somewhere. This is it—her own gun and the one that can be traced to her." His voice was a monotone. "But her own gun isn't the same one that put a bullet in my office wall—not any more. After Nell died, the killer did some reboring and scouring work inside the barrel—then cleaned it and put it away. The barrel markings are all different now. It can be done with a fine rattail file the right size."

Georgie shivered as though about to awake and Irene crooned to him.

Thursday said, "Ballistics will prove that this gun was not the one fired in my office. The gun that put the bullet in my wall and killed Colonel Fathom and killed Nell Kopke no longer exists. That mythical gun which I claimed as my own is the murder gun. Not this one in my hand—it's innocent because the barrel markings have been changed." He put the revolver away in his pocket suddenly and gazed through the windshield at nothing, trying to think. But it all came down to the same provable fact, the kind Benedict worshiped. "I claimed the gun that killed two people, and it can't be proved otherwise." He said it aloud.

Irene understood none of it. She held Georgie close and said again, "Poor child."

CHAPTER 31

SATURDAY, AUGUST 13 10:00 P.M.

He had Irene stop by the roadside on the outskirts of San Ysidro. While borderbound traffic streamed past, Thursday printed a rough-lettered note which he pinned to Georgie's shirt front.

The woman shook her head over the scrawny figure collapsed between them in sleep. "Oh, why must he ever wake up, Max? What he's been through is so horrible."

"He'll forget most of it. He's young enough."

"But what's going to happen to him?"

"Nothing good. The parents he had were on the fringe of the law, which is putting it nicely. Now they're both gone and he's an orphan—that means a state home. So he gets hit coming and going, heredity and environment." Thursday studied Irene's patrician profile hovering tenderly over the boy's mussed hair. "He's not a pretty kid, either. He won't appeal to adopters."

"He isn't ugly," she protested. "Little boys aren't supposed to be beautiful."

"That's easier to say when he's your own kid. But when you're shopping around you're particular. Adopters want them younger and cuter. No, Georgie'll grow up in a state home and, with the breaks he's gotten, he'll work his way through reform school right into a state prison."

"Oh, no!" She hugged the little body suddenly and Georgie whimpered in his sleep.

Thursday shrugged. "Maybe I'm getting morbid. I got state prisons on my mind tonight. Let's get on with what we got to do. After all, you can't take him back to the Benedict mansion."

She bit her lip and started the Buick up again. She followed his directions into the little town which fed off the border gates a mile south. Thursday had her stop in front of the county sheriff's substation. It was lighted but deserted. Through the steamy window of the short-order cafe next door he could see a bulky man in a visored cap at the counter. When the block was free of passers-by, Thursday scooped Georgie up and hurried into the substation. He left the sleeping boy on a bench inside the door and went back to the car. "Let's go."

"Will he be all right?" Irene asked, trying to get a last view of the youngster as they sped away.

"He's asleep and he's safe. I wish I could say the same."

"Where now, Max?"

"Coffee's place. North to Eighth Street in National City, then take Highland over to Federal Boulevard."

It was ten-thirty when they pulled up within the bleak framework of the former filling station. Thursday got out and rattled the door and presently a light came. After a brief conversation he passed Nell Kopke's .32 through a broken pane and slipped back into the car. "Your house. I got a big idea but I don't know what to do with it."

They sped off again through the lowering canyon sides. "Why'd you give the gun to Mr. Coffee?" Irene asked.

"I told him to file it into dust or melt it or anything to destroy it for once and all. You see, this frame I wandered into depends a lot on Nell's gun being found and being proved a different gun than the one I claimed in my office. The killer counted on the police finding Nell's changed gun rather than me finding it. So now Nell's gun will never be found in either form. There's no gun to support my story about her shot at me, but there's no gun to break my story, either. Which brings the odds up to fifty-fifty, anyway."

They rolled up the road between the avocado trees in nervous silence, but the big house looked the same as when they had left. The district attorney had not yet come home. Inside, Thursday hurried immediately to the radio in Benedict's study and tuned up the police calls. The search was county-wide now and tall thin men with arched noses were reported everywhere and being picked up everywhere.

"Quite a rat race," Thursday murmured. "Benedict's got his heart in this." He looked over at Irene in the doorway, her eyes hazily contemplating space. She hadn't bothered to take off her coat. "What are you thinking about?" he asked gently.

"Oh, several things. About Georgie and what you said. Max, I didn't realize you dwelt on subjects like that."

"Like what happens to other people?"

"I suppose so." She brought him into her gaze and drifted toward him. "You've really taught me a good many lessons. You're a pretty wonderful sort of person to discover, you know—a sort of cavalier *manqué*."

"You bet," he said and snorted. Then he put his hands on her arms to stop her advance. She tossed her head so the scarf fell back off her neat blonde hair. She raised her serious face and her lips were parted, expecting his. He said, "Irene, we're all strung tight tonight, and you especially are doing things you never did before. So don't let this chase feeling get you. Tomorrow you'll never believe it happened."

"Max..."

"Personally, I'm hungry. I been living on cigarettes all day. I hope your husband believes in food."

She twisted away and walked slowly to the door, bumping against a chair. "Thank you." A moment later she smiled wryly at him over her shoulder. "I forgot my manners, didn't I? We can raid the icebox if you'd like."

"Icebox dates you, Irene—or so I'm told. Refrigerator is what—" He stopped, frowning, head cocked toward the radio.

"What is it?" Irene asked.

Thursday listened to more of the metallic voice before he reduced the volume. "Don Kerner. Sounds like some Boy Scouts on an overnight hike found him out in Rose Canyon. Bludgeoned not over an hour ago—that's so it'd match the pattern of the Papago death. Two bludgeonings, two shootings, and I'll inherit them all."

"Don Kerner. He's—"

"Yeah. Well, your husband won't be interested in sleep tonight, that's for sure." He urged her out the door. "How about some food?"

He called Quincy's apartment again—no one answered—and then wandered out to the kitchen to watch Irene rummage through the refrigerator.

She asked, "Was that man important to you, Max?"

"Uh-huh. But I gave him up as soon as I heard he was out of jail. He undoubtedly knew what was coming, too, but he couldn't refuse bail without attracting attention and he was scared of his record. I didn't count on Quincy locating him but she did and—*what's that?*"

He leaped forward and clawed a bulky package out of the freezing compartment. It was wrapped in heavy buff-colored paper. His eyes accused the astonished Irene Benedict. "Where'd this come from?" He got the paper ripped open and inside was a small pot roast, frozen solid.

"Max—what are you doing?"

He put the icy roast on the sink and held its thick wrapping up to the light. The watermark read For Better Protection TITE. Comparison was unnecessary but he got the list out of his wallet, the list written on the kind of paper which had been lying around Rupert's office at Night & Day. The two papers were identical.

"Come on, Irene. Give. Where do they wrap meat this way?"

"It's only the usual paper. All my meat at the frozen food locker is wrapped in it. I took that roast out today for Sunday dinner. I don't—"

He was grinning broadly. "It's not usual to me. This shiny side is some sort of coated insulation. Do all the frozen food places use this?"

"I don't know. I've only been to the one here in La Mesa."

"Honey, I bet I know where your IOUs are—along with some dynamite that ought to change your husband's mind. Let's get back to that phone."

He raced down the hall to the study and dialed the *Sentinel* office. Merle Osborn's desk. She picked up her end after one ring. With only a terse explanation, he gave her instructions and hung up to wait. He couldn't sit still. He paced up and down, chewing his knuckles between cigarettes. Irene came in shortly with some bacon-and-tomato sandwiches and he stayed on his feet to eat them. She sat and watched him go back and forth. "Just one little bit of luck," he hoped aloud.

It was nearly a half hour before the phone jangled. Thursday let Irene answer and pass the receiver to him. Merle said, "Stinking news, Thursday."

"Don't say that. None at all?"

"Every one of the lockers is running to capacity since hot

weather started. They've been booked up since April at least. No new rentals this week."

He swore softly but savagely. Then, "I been getting too clever. Are you up to calling all the managers again?"

Merle groaned. "I had to get two of them out of bed. They'll hate me."

"But I won't, Osborn."

"If I can count on that, it's a deal. What do you want to know this time?"

"This. Has anybody named Rupert or Day had a food locker all along?"

"That's nice and vague. I'll call you."

Thursday went back to pacing. The scrap of paper from Night & Day pointed definitely to the blackmail goods having been hidden in a frozen food locker somewhere in the county. But there were a number of locker plants, and his time was short, and his freedom of movement limited by every prowl car. Without specific information. . . .

The more he thought it over the lower his spirits sank. When the telephone finally rang again at eleven-forty, he didn't even make a motion toward answering it. Irene said, holding it out to him, "It's the same woman."

"Hi, Osborn. What's the bad word?"

"You sound great. Are you sure you can stand glad tidings?"

"No fooling!" He gripped the receiver tightly. "Who and where?"

"Speaking of who, who is that woman answering your phone, might I ask?"

"A friend. Get to the word."

"Winter Weather Freezer in La Jolla, the last on my list, naturally. The manager's one of those with an early bedtime but he's been sweet about the whole thing. A Dartmouth man, he tells me. He invited me out to look at his icicles."

"You're not amusing me. What's the name and locker number?"

"You didn't tell me to get the locker number." He swore

and Merle chuckled. "Being a bright little reporter, I got it anyway. Number 509. It's rented by Miss Quincy Day. Happy?"

He laughed with relief. "Now you see why I'm as smug as you say. I got friends like you. Osborn, I could kiss you."

"Talk's cheap," she said and hung up.

Thursday slammed the phone together and laughed again. He said to Irene's excited face, "Let's make that twenty-mile trip to La Jolla. If this doesn't pay off, they keep a handy ocean there for guys who feel like jumping."

Chapter 32

SUNDAY, AUGUST 14, 12:15 A.M.

A little past midnight. Max Thursday stood on a sidewalk in La Jolla. Irene's car disappeared down Genter Street, going back the way she'd come. Even the coast breeze seemed warm to him tonight as he hesitated before testing his luck. It was pleasant to stand still, doing nothing to prove himself wrong, and listen to the distant grumble of the Pacific and the occasional spurting by of a car on the boulevard a block away.

The Winter Weather Freezer was out of the central commercial district of the rich seaside resort. In the dark its low-hanging roof and modern lines, with only a modest gold-letter sign, could be mistaken for just another large residence. It held aloof from the sidewalk, behind a smooth lawn and beds of nodding flowers.

Thursday snapped out of his inaction and strolled past the building, scrutinizing the broad plate-glass windows, hunting the easiest means of entrance. Irene had suggested that he have the manager let him in, but he had said no. What he intended to do—rifle a locker—could only be interpreted as burglary, no matter how worthy his purpose.

He reached the shadows behind the building and continued his search along a loading platform. The rear door was securely locked but next to it was a small window, unscreened. He ran his hand along the painted sill and a large sliver of wood pricked his thumb. Frowning, he pulled the fragment out and tried the lower half of the glass. The window slid up, rattling like an avalanche in his caution-tuned eardrums.

After a moment of straining silence, Thursday decided he wasn't going to hear anything else. He heaved his long body up and wriggled through the small opening. His blind hand groped over a worktable edge and he braced himself on that before lowering himself to the concrete floor. He half-crouched there, motionless, alert to something he couldn't define. Then he realized a cold draft had eddied around his ankles for a moment and ceased. While trying to remember its direction, he heard a door close softly. Somewhere ahead in the dark.

He could hear the blood pump faster in his head. The already-open window . . . He had arrived here immediately behind someone else.

Narrowing his eyes as if to will some semblance of form to the murky front part of the freezing plant, Thursday stole forward, groping for obstacles. Ahead of him, faintly, moon-light filtered through the plate-glass windows. His eyes improved with each step and he saw he was in a long wide corridor lined with meat blocks, enamel-top tables, and scales. He reached out toward the gleaming reflections of racked blades and selected a long, pointed carving knife. He began his slow advance along the corridor again.

His toe connected with something and a metal basket skittered away across the concrete, flipping over. In the instant of quiet which followed, Thursday held himself rigid. Then there was a rush of light footsteps and the clash of bolts and the creak of a heavy door opening.

Thursday charged forward, leading with the knife. It was turned aside violently and his shoulder smashed into the massive hardwood door of the plant's refrigeration room. Icy air bathed his face. He caught the door before it closed completely and slipped into the absolute blackness of the huge meat box.

He eased the door to behind him without letting it latch. As he did so, a second heavy door clicked shut at the far end of the box. He moved toward the noise, his hands found the surface of the door, found the latch. He shoved. Unbelieving, he threw his weight against the smooth, iron latch handle again. He dropped his knife and tried a third time.

The door was locked or jammed from the outside.

Thursday felt a sickening coldness that had nothing to do with the flood of bitter air churning down from above. He stumbled quickly back the way he'd come. The first door was now tight shut, too, and neither would its handle budge under his pounding.

Then he began really to feel the cold. It wrapped him round like a blanket and penetrated deeper and deeper as if peeling off successive layers of his flesh. And he couldn't see anything. It was worse because he couldn't see.

As if granting a wish, fluorescent lights overhead flickered and chattered and came to life. He spun around watchfully but he was alone in the box, alone in the twelve-by-eight room, its varnished planks flecked with sparkling snow. All about him, sides of beef and lamb and pork and venison hung from wall hooks, and a row of metal baskets held packages wrapped in the familiar buff-colored paper. But neither the slaughtered animals nor he had turned on the lights.

There was the door at one end he had entered, and a door at the other which presumably led to the public locker room at the front of the plant. Otherwise . . . His eyes leaped to an opening midway along the wall, the size of a small picture frame. His panic-born hopes died immediately. The aperture was large enough for a good-sized cat to pass through—or a parcel of meat—but far too small an exit for even a small man.

His heart jumped again at the sound of a latch being raised. But the noise came from the parcel opening and Quincy Day's voice called. "Max?" hollowly.

He got to one side of the opening and bent to peek through quickly. It was a wooden tunnel nearly as long as his arm and he figured it would logically open into the preparation corridor. He hadn't seen anything at the other end. Quincy's husky voice said again, "Max?"

"Oh, I'm here," Thursday said. "Satisfied?"

"You shouldn't have come."

"Skip it. Now, are you going to use your head and unlock one of those doors?"

She paused. "I don't know."

"I wasn't asking you, Quincy. You couldn't have worked that door stunt alone. I was asking your boss, the Night of Night & Day. How about it, Vespasian?"

Joaquin Vespasian's staccato laugh came in from the outer darkness. "Say, I think you just answered your own question, Maxie."

"You're missing some angles, you know that. The cops are on their way here right now. Let me out before they catch me here and maybe we can make a deal."

"You're lousy at lying. You got nothing to deal with. Nothing big enough. Maybe if you hadn't been so chintzy back when you thought I was a small-time grifter—boy, were you big and tough, then!"

"Okay. This place still opens at eight o'clock. Sundays included."

"So you'll still be here. Maxie, old friend, the temperature in that box is some twenty below zero. A beef carcass freezes solid in an hour or so. So you'll walk around for maybe two hours before you get sleepy. And that's that."

Thursday didn't answer at once, waiting to make certain his voice would come out sounding normal. "Quincy," he called. "Two other people know I came here tonight to look through your food locker. You leave me here and you're tied to me forever."

"Max, I don't want to leave you, of course," Quincy said. "But Joaquin is absolutely right. We must think of ourselves."

"Sure, but think of your own self first. If you still have the key to your locker, hang on to it. Vespasian's always kept himself out of things, you notice. You're the next one being rigged, sweetheart."

Vespasian swore scoffingly with a voice that strutted.

Thursday grimaced painfully, trying to think of a wedge. Unless he could beat them with talk.... He jammed his hands in his pockets and chased the *unless* out of his mind. Through his pockets his palms felt the chilled skin of his thighs. He thrust again at the pair outside with "Quincy, you're still pretty much in the clear. They can nail your boy friend with two of the four killings, but you don't actually face a murder rap—yet."

A moment of silence from the other end of the little tunnel. Then Quincy whispered something and Vespasian answered sharply, "Don't let him kid you, Quincy." He raised his voice to Thursday, "She's been in half of everything since I set up Night & Day for her in '44. She's been front and I been brains."

"It sure looks it," Thursday said. "When Rupert, her doctor stooge, got out of prison he slid into a nice clean job across the room from her. But you stayed in that ratty plaster shack, telling fortunes. That's brains, huh?"

"You know how the cops pick off big guys? They see they got more flash than the day before when they were little guys. So I stayed safe as a little guy where I could move around more. Besides, any time I wanted, I could relax, enjoy the good things I earned."

"You mean Quincy," Thursday said. He shivered and his

cheek brushed the cold skinned corpse of a lamb. He began talking again, afraid to let the conversation lag. They might go away. They might turn off the lights. "So that shaving gear in her apartment belonged to you and not to Rupert like she let me think. I guess you were up there with her the night Fathom got cute and killed Papago."

"Fathom." Vespasian sounded as if he'd just spit. "He had rocks for brains. Papago could have been bought off or fenced in. Killing him was dumb."

"You bet it was. That's what probably kept you in business so long, steering clear of downright murder. You weren't cut out for it. You'd rather scheme around things. Like that first night when you planted the hat in my car and Papago's body among the alligators. Fear tactics—you're good at that."

"I like to use what's lying around," Vespasian said. "I got right next to you after you rang me in with that hat. You had me worried for a few hours there, until I found out you were just chasing anybody connected with the Greek. And you had me worried tonight when I heard you had broken loose from the D.A. I called your office, thought we might get together on that phony deal we were always going to make. I didn't want you staying loose, I got to admit. Never know what you might do next. Up to now."

Thursday managed a sort of laugh. "What if I'd tabbed you earlier? I might have hitched you to the shakedown business just because of your taste in women. You went for Rosa Lalli and Nell Kopke, both big women. What if I'd figured a little squirt like you might be next to Quincy who's also on the large side?"

"But you shouldn't have stayed alive past Wednesday, Maxie. *I* sent Nell up to see you at your office. She depended on me quite a bit and after her lover-boy got his, she was open to suggestions for revenge. I suggested you in a round-about way, but her shooting wasn't all she claimed it was."

"Yeah, and you believing her bragging put you in the hospital."

"I thought that had the makings of a pretty fair setup myself. There was Nell's bullet in your office wall, with a good chance it could be dug out and identified. And here was Colonel Fathom, making noises like he was somebody important. If I could talk Nell into shooting Fathom with a gun you had said was yours—see? Setup. I even changed Nell's bullets from lead ones to nickel-jackets. Nickel slugs get marked up less by the gun barrel but, if they hit a bone, there's less chance of them getting mashed useless for identification. And, Maxie, it paid off."

Thursday found he was shivering violently now. He began to stamp his feet and move his shoulders back and forth, trying to warm as many muscles as possible without leaving the speaking tube. "Only trouble was the way it worked out. You didn't mind *me* being with Fathom in the line of fire. But I made *you* sit in the front seat with the target, and Nell did her usual blind shooting. Fathom was putting on a scared act before that, wasn't he? You told him it was a trap for me, didn't you?"

Quincy's voice cut in, "You didn't say that, did you, Joaquin?"

"Sure he did, Quincy. Are you sure of his plans for you, by the way? I bet he's even started carrying a gun now. He's killed two people tonight, and it's easy to get the habit."

Vespasian snapped at her, "Fathom doesn't matter. Forget him."

"Nell Kopke trusted you for a while and now she doesn't matter," Thursday insisted silkily. "You laid out a nice train alibi for her, Vespasian. Why didn't she leave town the second time? Why'd she stick around and get mad at you?"

"The bottle was getting her, Maxie. Nothing she wanted more than to get the guy who got Papago—until after she'd done it. Then she couldn't stand the idea of having killed somebody and started blaming me. What you call a guilt complex."

"And you finally had to do a killing personally. I was down

to San Ysidro earlier tonight, Vespasian. Up till I found that rebored .32, I'd thought the frame for Fathom's murder was only unlucky coincidences. But Nell's revolver made me see different. It made me see that her bullet in my wall wasn't exactly discovered by the D.A.'s man—it was pointed out to him by Yvonne Odler. It made me see that the brains behind such a frame had to be Nell or somebody she talked to. And you were the guy she generally let her hair down for."

Vespasian didn't seem to be listening any longer. Thursday could hear him murmuring to the woman, something about "leaving" and "key."

Thursday said. "Quincy! What about it?"

Again she hesitated. "Max, I hate to. But I must."

The little man asked through the opening. "You want the lights left on or off?"

Thursday fought back the fear that wanted to smother his voice. "Vespasian, you better listen to a few details—even if your girl friend won't. You're not the only schemer in your outfit. Quincy has had a few ideas, too. Like moving all the goods out here without telling you about it."

"What makes you think she didn't tell me?" Vespasian asked edgily.

"Remember when I sent you up to break into Night & Day? You figured Don Kerner had already named some names to me, and it wouldn't do much harm to bring me back your actual sucker list. That'd also make you look good to me for a little longer, while you spun the rest of your web. But you picked up that scrap of frozen food paper in Rupert's office where he'd wrapped up the goods for transfer. No, you'd never have written the list on that particular piece of paper if you'd known what Quincy had done. And she didn't tell you about the move very long ago either, or you wouldn't have waited until this late hour to get the stuff out."

"Doesn't hold water, Maxie. I was in the hospital, out of commission. Quincy did what she thought best."

"Certainly," the woman's voice chimed in quickly. "I'm glad you understand that, Joaquin."

"Do you understand why she sent Rupert up to blast you with that shotgun, Vespasian?"

Silence began and blossomed. Quincy's tense voice killed it. "Don't listen to him, Joaquin. You know he's merely bluffing, attempting to save himself. You know it was Kerner."

Thursday laughed, trying to sound scornfully confident. His jaw ached from keeping his teeth from chattering. "That Kerner story's a hot one. Get this, Vespasian—Don Kerner was in jail up till this morning. I know because I parked him there personally. He couldn't have put that buckshot in you. But Rupert could and would and did. You think he likes your guts because you've got Quincy and he hasn't any more?"

Then he heard Vespasian's whisper. "Quincy—let me see your face."

"Clever girl." Thursday kept stabbing at them. "She's cut the corners pretty fine but she thought of every possibility. As soon as the radio news told her you'd gone to the hospital, Vespasian, she called me up for a breakfast date. She buttered me up, entertained me that whole next day. She wanted the protection of my big strong arms, in case I ended up with all the cards. Meanwhile, she had your blackmail property moved to make sure I wouldn't get hold of that. And the same day she tried to get you polished off so she could have the whole works. Then when she found Kerner was in jail, she had Rupert spring him, just so you'd have a goat for that shotgun blast."

"No," Quincy said. "He's lying. Obviously."

"Obviously," Vespasian said. "On the other hand, you always brag about that time in Cleveland when you let Rupert take your tumble. Turn on your flashlight, Quincy. I want to see your face when you tell me."

"You see, Vespasian, you really didn't have to crack Kerner's skull for him. He didn't want anything but out. He'd never—"

"Quincy—let's have that light!"

"Get away from me," her voice went up shrilly. "Get away from me! Don't ever forget you're not the only one with a gun!"

"I got to know that he's lying, don't I?"

"Joaquin, if you don't trust me—I warn you—"

"The light, Quincy girl. And give me the locker key. If you don't get a move on, I'm going to come and—"

A shot thundered through the building. Thursday flattened against the meat box wall, keeping away from the opening. He heard another shot, another, and then four more strung together like firecrackers. Glass fell musically, an overture to the silence.

Then his ears caught the soft bump as somebody sank to the corridor floor outside. "Vespasian!" he called. "Quincy!"

Neither answered, and he called again. After a moment, he heard footsteps move slowly away toward the front of the plant. He heard the feet crunch through glass, and then there was no more sound. The door to the parcel tunnel drifted to, and his outstretched arm couldn't catch it before it clicked shut.

Thursday began walking swiftly back and forth, flailing his arms. Overhead, the vents hissed biting wind down on him. He lit a cigarette to warm his stiff hands a little but the suck of smoke pained his throat. He stomped it out.

On the other side of the wall, in the preparation corridor, someone lay. Quincy or Vespasian? Dead or alive? He scrubbed his hands together and could barely feel the contact. Seven shots. Had any of them been heard? He said aloud, "Not much point in me making them fight if nobody's going to hear the noise." He didn't like the sound of his voice.

He thought things, instead. He thought, pretty proud of yourself, aren't you? And, somebody's bound to let you out before long.

Thursday stamped around helplessly, looking at the frozen meat on the hooks and wondering.

Chapter 33

SUNDAY, AUGUST 14, 2:00 A.M.

Austin Clapp stepped through the broken front window of the Winter Weather Freezer and crossed the lawn to where a police intern was walking Thursday up and down. "How are you feeling now, Max?"

Thursday still shivered spasmodically, even beneath the two ponderous army blankets clutched around his body. He still couldn't feel the soles of his feet or his fingertips. His lungs ached from nearly an hour of the subzero air, and he sneezed and they ached worse. He muttered, "I'm dying."

Clapp grinned sympathetically. "Maybe next time you'll think it over before you take on a gang single-handed, bright boy. Maybe you'll remember the pasting you took for nothing."

Thursday snorted. "Go on. Pull the old one about going into a battle of wits half-armed."

The homicide chief fell into step with Thursday and the intern as they paraded up and down the sidewalk, past the parked prowl cars and motorcycles. The ambulance had pulled in by the rear loading platform. Slippered, robed, and staring neighbors had come out of the Genter Street houses to guess what was going on. Clapp sighed. "The story I got from the victim inside clears you of the murder charge pretty well. All that's left against you are a few felonies."

"A half hour ago I didn't care."

"You better start caring. And thinking. I talked to Benedict on the radio. Because of this handful of new business, he says to let you stay free on recognizance for a while. He's going to attend to you later."

Thursday frowned. "I think he's got a better reason than what he laughingly calls my recognizance."

"What?"

Thursday didn't answer. He said, "Poor Benedict. He worked so hard for my execution, too." They grinned at each other.

Clapp said, "Even funnier than Benedict is you getting caught among the ice cubes tonight."

"I told you. I got in touch with Vespasian and he said meet him on this corner. Why this particular corner I'll never know. Then he pulled up with Quincy Day in her car and took a potshot at me. It broke that window and since I didn't have a gun I dove inside and hid in the icebox. They couldn't get in to me so they fixed it that I wouldn't get out. Then Quincy and Vespasian had a fight and—"

"Sure, sure. It still makes you look pretty silly." Clapp glanced over Thursday's shrouded figure. "Feel like going back inside now?"

"Am I wanted?"

"Uh-huh. Doc Stein says you better hurry."

Thursday shook out of the two blankets and gave them to the intern. With Clapp, he returned to the locker plant through the big smashed window. They pushed through the milling uniforms and plainclothesmen and ambulance men into the brilliantly lighted preparation corridor. Police cameras were flashing. Stein was at the telephone.

The stretcher lay along an enamel-top wrapping table, a scale at its head. Thursday leaned over the woman and touched her clenched fist. Quincy Day opened her slant eyes and smiled up weakly. The lipstick was chewed from her mouth. She whispered, "I'm so glad you came back, darling."

"How you feeling, Quincy?"

"Fine. They gave me something. How are you, Max?"

"Don't worry about me. I'm okay."

"I'm so glad. I didn't want to leave you in there. You know I didn't want to, don't you?"

"Sure, I knew you didn't."

"I would have come back to let you out. I had planned—" Her pale lips trembled and she insisted, "You do believe me, Max?"

"I believe you, honey."

"Darling. That's good." Her eyes drifted shut, and the only darkness on her chalky face was in her winged eyebrows.

"Quincy?"

Stein tapped Thursday's shoulder and drew him a step away. He said, low-voiced, "We're taking her down the road to Scripps Hospital. I'm afraid it's a waste of time but we got to make the effort."

"Bad off?"

"Three times through the abdomen, close up. She'd lost a lot of blood by the time I got here and the hemorrhage—there's no way to stop it in time."

"Stein," said Thursday, "do you mind if I ride to the hospital with her?"

"Why should I? Put the interns up front if you like." He motioned to the ambulance crew.

When they lifted the stretcher. Quincy spread her eyes wide, frightened. "Max!" she called. "Where are you?"

"Right here, Quincy." He walked along with one hand on the stretcher as they carried it through the building, across the loading platform, and into the black police ambulance.

"This is no time to leave," she whispered. When he crouched beside her and the doors shut them in alone, she twisted her mouth into a colorless grin. "So much left unsaid and now I can hardly talk at all." The pallor gave her a girlish look; there was no longer anything of the witch about her. Her two fists lay tightly gripped on her breast, outside the blanket.

He clumsily smoothed the hair off her forehead. He felt the ambulance turn around and creep along the driveway to the street. Quincy was watching his face. "Max . . ."

"Right beside you, honey."

"I really think I'm through now. Isn't that so?"

He lied. "No. The doc says you'll come out all right. It's better if you just relax."

She tried to raise her head and couldn't. "Max—you did care, didn't you? That's what counts, your caring quite a bit.

You wouldn't have sent me to prison if you could possibly have saved me, would you? You'd have thought of something, I meant so much to you."

His pause was hardly noticeable before he lied again. "That's right, honey. I would have let you get away."

Quincy smiled, satisfied, and let her head loll to one side. Thursday took up one clenched fist and gently opened the curled fingers. He spread the hand out on the blanket and lifted the other fist. Quincy rolled her head back to him again. Her violet eyes fluttered open, shut, then open. He could barely hear her say, "You may have the key, darling."

She opened her fingers, and the locker key slid out on the blanket. It lay glinting silvery for a moment before Thursday picked it up. Quincy still smiled up at him, her exotic eyes unblinking.

When they reached the receiving entrance of Scripps Hospital, Thursday was still crouched beside her, holding a hand that seemed as cold as his own.

CHAPTER 34

SUNDAY, AUGUST 14 AND MONDAY, AUGUST 15

For the next two days, Max Thursday remained at large and busy. Every time he sneezed, he thought of Benedict. He was expecting re-arrest momentarily but it didn't come. He knew why Benedict was holding off—and it wasn't because Thursday had relinquished credit for the Night & Day case.

The *Sentinel* extra, Sunday morning, gave over the entire front page to Merle Osborn's flamboyant story of "the fall of the blackmail empire." The *Sentinel* editors knew a beat when it fell in their laps—and they owned one in Merle's pictures, the complete set she had taken of Night & Day personnel and interiors following the pretended robbery.

So that edition was only the first of three extras erupted by the *Sentinel* presses during those two days, setting a record for even that paper's gaudy career. The second, hawked through a baking Sunday afternoon, was about Rupert. The third, at breakfast time Monday, was about Vespasian.

Rupert, formerly Dr. Theodore Newman of Cleveland, shot himself in a room of the Liberty Hotel after hearing the first radio report of Quincy's death. He left a rambling note which blamed Vespasian for the murders of Papago, Fathom, Kerner, and Nell Kopke. He did his best to absolve Quincy of all guilt. His room was cluttered with pictures of the slant-eyed woman, and souvenirs—dozens of handkerchiefs, the single letter she had written him in prison, old theater programs, and even a compact with a broken mirror. Rupert, using his left hand because of a broken trigger finger on his right, fumbled the first attempt but reached his heart with the second.

Joaquin Vespasian had nearly reached Albuquerque by dawn Monday. He was buying gasoline at a combination filling station and roadside cafe when a young deputy sheriff finished his coffee and stepped outside. Vespasian, feverish and bleary-eyed, reacted to the sight of the uniform by drawing his gun. His fusillade went wild but the deputy's reply didn't. The autopsy revealed that, in addition to the bullet which killed him, Vespasian's small body also held four slugs from Quincy's automatic and several pellets from Rupert's attempted assassination. And his earlier wounds from Nell Kopke's revolver were festering with infection.

"Beats me how he got so far," Clapp told Thursday on the telephone Monday noon. "But that winds up the homicide end. I'm satisfied even if Benedict isn't."

"Was he ever?"

"He's tearing his remaining hair over the blackmail stuff. They had to have a file somewhere but he can't find it. Last night he impounded that whole freezer out in La Jolla and spent most of the night opening packages of meat. Quincy Day had a locker there, all right, but it was empty."

"If I were the vindictive type, I'd wish him as bad a cold as I got."

"I've heard you in better voice. It getting you down?"

"I chiseled Stein out of some city penicillin. He's got a crazy idea I'll live."

"You better. Benedict wants to see you this afternoon." Clapp paused. "However, it's not an order, Max. Just an invitation. Want to go?"

"Pick me up about four. I'll be tied up till then."

Thursday had spent all Monday morning and would spend most of the afternoon delivering Night & Day's extortion material and Kerner's photostatic copies to the rightful owners. In each case, he insisted that they destroy the evidence in his presence.

He had made his only exception of Irene Whitney Benedict. He had destroyed the ten IOUs himself, after Merle Osborn, using Quincy's key, opened the locker Sunday morning. He had immediately phoned a terse message to Irene and received a brief thank-you.

Now, after Clapp hung up, he extracted a flat little package from among the morning mail on his desk. The La Mesa postmark had caught his eye and he knew it was from Irene. Thursday cut open the paper, cleared the ribbon out of his way, and sat grinning down at the open gift box. He examined the contents. There were fifteen ten-dollar bills, the balance of his fee for six days. There was no message, but the money was inserted in the leather wallet she had been making for her husband. It was finished.

Shortly after four, he and Clapp were ushered by Ed Wales into the district attorney's office. Wales gave Thursday an especially friendly smile and then left the visitors alone with Benedict.

Benedict didn't smile. His long face stayed neutral, gazing across the desks as if Thursday's chair were still empty. "It is in some part through your efforts, Thursday, that we have destroyed a vicious organization. Although some aspects of the case don't satisfy this office, a broad sort of justice seems to have been done."

"Nothing ever turns out quite the way you expect," Thursday murmured. He put a coughdrop in his mouth. "By the way, I understand congratulations are in order for you." Benedict raised his eyebrows. "I read this morning about you starting adoption proceedings on Georgie Papago."

"That's a fine thing, Benedict," Clapp rumbled.

"Yes." But the district attorney didn't seem completely pleased as his eyes dropped to Irene's picture. "Thank you for your congratulations, but in all honesty I must tell you it was my wife who insisted that the youngster deserved this opportunity. I'll pass your words along to her."

Benedict appraised Thursday again. "However . . . Perhaps Lieutenant Clapp has told you that the material used for extortion by the Night & Day group has not been found."

"Probably Vespasian destroyed it when you started to close in. Anyway, if it's gone it's not going to hurt anybody."

"If it is gone. In view of your methods, I was hoping you could shed some light on the situation."

Thursday sucked on his coughdrop. "Come out and say it."

"I dislike to make a direct accusation, Thursday, so I'll put it as a question. Are you for any reason hiding this evidence?"

Thursday looked at Clapp. "Your idea of a friendly call?" Clapp shrugged and kept his mouth shut. Thursday said, "Benedict, if you feel like making an official charge I'll be glad to hand you an official answer. Until then, you can think what you like."

"Perhaps you've forgotten how many charges are pending against you already. Escape from detention, assault upon a duly empowered—"

"I haven't forgotten."

Benedict stood up slowly. "Then you may guess how strongly I'm tempted."

Thursday rose at the same time. He chewed up his cough

drop, swallowed the fragments, and said, "Look. I know exactly why you haven't thrown the book at me. You can't find the Night & Day stuff and you're afraid I got it. You're afraid my going to jail might send that dirty linen straight to a laundry called the *Sentinel*."

Clapp said, "I'm not present," and ambled to the door. He asked Benedict, "Is he free to go or isn't he?" When neither man answered him, he went on out.

The other two fought it out with their eyes, estimating, judging. Thursday spoke first. "What I said. That's it, isn't it?"

Then he waited. His freedom, his license depended on Benedict. On how stubborn the man was. On—Thursday didn't like the thought—whether such a man, devoted to honesty, could be bribed.

Finally, Benedict said coolly, "That's it precisely, a matter of balance." His face was stiff. "I can forego punishing you, Thursday, only because that action might harm far more valuable members of the community. You see, I've estimated your character correctly." He nodded dismissal and sat down to work among the papers on his desk.

"You're a lousy gambler, Benedict. I might be bluffing."

"No. I know you."

As Thursday reached the door, Benedict added, "But where we're leaving this matter extends only to this instant. Never forget that. I owe you nothing whatsoever."

"Sure. We'll start from scratch."

Thursday blew out his breath as he joined Clapp on the sunny courthouse steps. Clapp said, "Well, you got away with it all around, Max. Complete victory."

"I wouldn't say complete." Thursday murmured. "You called it right. There's a taste in my mouth."